The Last Draw

By the same author

Blood on the Saddle
The Comanche's Ghost
Blood Pass
The West Witch
Wanted
Ghost-Town Duel
The Gallows Ghost
The Widow Maker
Guns of the Past
Palomita

The Last Draw

LANCE HOWARD

A Black Horse Western

ROBERT HALE · LONDON

© Howard Hopkins 1999
First published in Great Britain 1999

ISBN 0 7090 6419 5

Robert Hale Limited
Clerkenwell House
Clerkenwell Green
London EC1R 0HT

Photoset in North Wales by
Derek Doyle & Associates, Mold, Flintshire.
Printed and bound in Great Britain by
WBC Book Manufacturers Limited, Bridgend.

To BZN for wonderful music . . .

ONE

Jack Trombley slapped his cards on the green felt-covered table and let out a curse that would have set the most hardened bar dove to blushing. An expression akin to reaching into a hole jam-packed with peeled rattlers struck his anvil-shaped face. Bloodshot smoky eyes narrowed and foam flecked the corners of his mouth. The cards – a straight – fanned out, an eight cartwheeling to the sawdust-covered floor.

'Jumpin' Christamighty, you cheated me, you lowly hornswoggler!' Jack's face turned livid and the words spat out with as much venom as one of those rattlers.

Luke Banner lifted his head, an effort, considering the way he felt. His cold grey eyes narrowed. He struggled to focus, vision clouded by a gauze of rotgut. He glanced at the scattered cards and chips lying helter-skelter in a pile, then at his own hand, which brimmed with enough aces to make a card-sharp turn hand-springs.

'I didn't cheat you, gent.' Banner's voice came low, even, with a trace of a slur and subtle threat. Many a man claimed it always carried that threat; he reckoned they were right to say it.

Many a dead man.

Trombley's face went a shade redder and with the

7

back of his hand he wiped the spittle away from his lips. 'Hell and tarnation you didn't, you lowly sumbitch! I seen you slip that ace outta your sleeve. I shoulda knowed your type cain't be trusted.' More spit gathered at the corners of Trombley's mouth like a church woman at a Saturday fair. Beads of sweat sprang out on his brow.

Under any other circumstances Banner might have laughed – in another life, one where his existence didn't depend on avoiding such affronts. Instead something dark twisted in his belly and his fingers twitched. A shiver of intent wiped a handful of the gauze from his mind and his cold gaze focused on the gambler's face. Jack Trombley was a stove to call the kettle; the gambler was a tinhorn with too much mustard, practiced – but not practiced enough – in the fine art of one-eyed poker-playing and Banner had welcomed a chance to trim his tree. 'Cept the fellow didn't take kindly to his lessons, especially after dropping the third hand in a row.

Drawing a slow breath, Banner tried to size up the man, but found himself saddled with conflicting conclusions. Most tinhorns would have backed down against Banner, fully knowing what he was – the Devil in Stetson, as one pulp writer had tagged him, slow fire and lightning triggered. But Trombley didn't have that spark of rabbit in his eyes. No, not at all. Oh, Banner saw fear, sure enough, ever so slight and gilded with bravado. But not enough. Not damn near enough, and not the type that made a man pocket his pride and turn tail. That told Banner he had misjudged the man, made subtle miscalculations based on a half-empty whiskey bottle and foolish complacency when the very nature of his presence in Bellstar should have prevented that.

You're slipping. You should have seen this man ain't no tinhorn. Not long ago you would have. . . .

Trombley's hand twitched and slid two inches towards the edge of the table.

Banner sobered a bit more. Now he felt sure Trombley was much more than just some tinhorn with his britches in a twist over losing.

Banner slowly laid his cards on the table. He wanted no sudden moves, because there was still a chance he could defuse the situation.

Do you really want to?

'Gent, I'm tellin' you plain I didn't cheat you. You best take my word for it and keep your hands where I can see 'em.' Banner's gaze flicked to the man's hand then back to his face. He drilled him with a steady gaze, fighting to keep his senses from swimming at the same time. Despite himself, his hand felt a shiver of anticipation and his heart stepped up a beat. Why was Trombley challenging him over this? The pot wasn't worth a notch over a hundred greenbacks and some loose silver. Was that worth a man's life?

Was anything?

Trombley's lips twitched, and a look came into his eyes, a look that asked the same question about life and worth and whether he had bitten off more than he cared to chew. Banner could see the man wanted to jerk his hand free of that rattlesnake hole, but also saw the tinhorn had decided it was either too late or that something bigger forced his decision in a deadly direction.

Trombley's lips twitched again and his sneer came forced. 'You best not be wantin' to walk out them doors with that pot, mister, not 'less you want an extra hole in your hide.'

That was it. Trombley had stepped across the line

and made intent an honest-to-boots threat and Banner would be forced to meet it. A sick feeling cinched in his belly and he relived a hundred such incidents in the course of a second. Gunfire and blue smoke, bodies and ruby blood. Death. It always ended the same for Luke Banner and he was damned tired of it.

Banner let out a deep sigh. 'Don't want no trouble with you, gent. Just wanted me a friendly poker game and I reckon I made a mistake playin' with a sore loser.'

You're goading him, you sonofabitch. . . .

Judas Priest! What the hell was wrong with him? Why couldn't he control the bastard dark thing welling inside, the dark soul that needed to punish and exact revenge?

Because you can't stop it any more. Maybe you never could. It's too powerful and it will kill you.

Didn't matter.

It never mattered. Because though there was a chance to stop it he could not and had for all intents made it inevitable, perhaps from the instant he sat at the table to play cards with this man.

A showdown. Wanted or not, it was what he was getting. Again. Always. Asked for or by circumstance.

Trombley's expression hardened. Sweat streaked down his face. Tobacco-stained teeth clenched and balls of muscle stood out at either side of his jaw.

Banner tensed, keenly aware he had tilted the odds – if indeed they were there to be tilted and he had doubts – to a violent end. Perhaps his own.

Trombley's voice lowered a notch, and came with a hint of a tremble. 'Hell of a thing to say, Banner. You best take a notion to swallow it.'

Trombley didn't wait for the retraction. The tinhorn's hand jerked into motion, streaking towards the edge of the table and Banner glimpsed a number of things flashing in the fellow's eyes – the man had planned this for some reason. He wanted to challenge Banner – or *had* too – and may have even lost on purpose. He wanted Banner to go for his gun and he wanted to see Banner lying in blood and sawdust on the saloon floor. The only question was why and that would have no time to be answered.

Trombley's hand dropped off the table and swooped towards his hip, where a Smith & Wesson rested in a tooled leather holster.

Banner's hand shot sideways, too, but not to the Peacemaker nestled in its greased holster at his side. He had one chance to undo the damage he had just provoked and he would take it.

He grasped the table edge and heaved. The move wasn't graceful but it caught Trombley by surprise. The table flew up and greenbacks and cards sailed to the floor. Poker chips clattered on the boards like colored snow. The table flew up and crashed into the tinhorn, whose hand never reached his gun.

Trombley catapulted backwards over his chair, table chasing him. Landing flat on his back, the tinhorn threw both hands up and shoved, sending the table sideways with a horrendous racket.

All noise in the crowded saloon ceased. Men stopped shouting and guffawing and swearing, and bargirls clipped their Lorelei giggles. The plinkety piano crashed to a jangling halt. Heads swiveled in the direction of the commotion.

Trombley bellowed a string of curses that threatened to peel the red-flower papering from the wall and tried to scramble to his feet.

Banner sprang from his chair without a smidgen of grace, hesitating a fraction as the room shimmied. His chair toppled over. His legs wobbled and he fought to gain his balance.

The faltering allowed Trombley to reach his feet and straighten. He swiped blood from his nose, which looked considerably flatter than it had before it smacked the table.

On instinct, Banner stumblingly threw himself forward, slamming into the tinhorn before the man had a chance to set himself completely and go for his iron.

The move was entirely clumsy, nothing he could be proud of, but it worked. He hit the fellow hard and took him backwards.

Trombley crashed into the bar and blew out a grunt and most of the foul air inhabiting his lungs. The gambler spat at Banner and cursed, fighting to get to his gun.

Banner banged his forehead into Trombley's already smashed nose and a geyser of crimson spurted out. The move hurt like hell, even in Banner's semi-stewed condition, but it was the only way to stop Trombley from reaching his piece. Banner had two handfuls of the gambler's frock coat and Trombley might have shot Banner's balls off before the manhunter got the chance to stop him.

Trombley bellowed like a castrated bull and hurled himself forward. Banner, still struggling with his balance, stumbled backward, but retained his grip on Trombley's coat.

The tinhorn staggered along with Banner like a clumsy hurdy-gurdy gal following a lush's lead. The manhunter tripped over a chair and pitched backward, the gambler in tow.

Banner struck the floor hard, air exploding from his lungs, the tinhorn coming down on top of him.

His head bounced on the floorboards just hard enough to stun him and send stars careening across his vision. Trombley's bulk felt like a cow stepping on his chest.

Trombley launched a punch and Banner instinctively jerked his head sideways, but not enough to avoid the blow completely. It sent more colored stars flashing before his eyes, and as the stars vanished the room whirled.

You're going to die. . . .

The thought crashed into his mind:, clearing away the befuddlement and he was in motion. A sudden lightness told Banner Trombley had climbed off his chest. Through blurred vision he saw the man scrambling backwards and to his feet. Banner forced himself up as the tinhorn came to a jerky stop.

'Hell with you, Banner!' the man yelled and his hand flashed for the Smith & Wesson.

Everything around him froze. He swore the cold specter of Death strolled through the batwings. He clearly saw the man's hand glide as if in slow motion towards the pistol. Saw it, registered it, and returned the perception of threat back to his own hand.

Banner was half up, crouched, really, but it was enough. His hand swooped for the Peacemaker.

A heartbeat.

Two.

The bastard comfort of the wooden grip in his hand.

For an instant he wasn't quite certain what had happened. He heard a shot and knew the gambler had fired.

He braced for the burning punch of lead drilling into his body, but instead felt a searing shriek of pain across his left biceps. The gambler had panicked upon seeing the manhunter go for the draw – not much, but enough to jerk the trigger instead of feathering it. That mistake saved Banner's life.

Another shot, a hair behind the first, Banner's Peacemaker. Though the man had drawn faster it was the manhunter whose aim was accurate.

Banner's gaze was nailed to the gambler and he saw a startled expression slap the fellow's hard features. A hole appeared in his chest as if by magic and spouted crimson. The man collapsed as if a puppeteer had suddenly dropped the strings. His pistol twirled across the floor.

Banner had no doubt the man was dead; he didn't need to go over and check. He just knew, as he always knew.

The air seemed to grow more chilled and he swore he heard Death laugh beside him. He shuddered, a sick feeling twisting in his belly as he stared at the dead form, the outstretched fingers that still twitched, the Smith & Wesson lying a few feet away.

Maybe next time. . . .

Yes, maybe next time. Maybe next time it would be him lying there, *his* blood seeping into the worn wood. It damn near had been.

You should have stopped it. You had a choice. You asked for this. You always ask for it. You can't bring her back. . . .

A noise sounded to his left and he turned his head to see a man step through the batwings, a somber expression saddling his jowly face.

Marshal Esidiah Hart glanced at Banner, the somberness turning a shade darker, mixing with grim resignation, and removed his hat. His gaze went to the dead man and he nudged his head at the body.

'What the hell happened here, Banner?' His voice came steady and without accusation.

Banner kept silent, the leaden feeling of death still weighing on him. He barely heard the marshal's query.

'Banner?' The marshal moved closer, eyes narrowing.

Banner gazed at him, taking a slow breath and sliding his Peacemaker into its holster. 'Marshal . . .' His words faltered and for one of the few times in his life he thought he might actually just collapse into the closest chair.

You're slipping more and more, Banner, losing your speed and control and it is only a matter of time till you're lying boots up.

The marshal ran a hand through his thinning hair. 'Asked what happened, Banner. I expect an answer.' The marshal went to the dead man and scooched, hand going to the fellow's neck, checking for a sign of life. He turned back and looked up at the manhunter. 'Dead. . .'

Banner nodded, a grim turn on his lips.

The marshal straightened and stepped back to Banner. 'You plannin' on answerin' me?' It was no longer a request.

Banner peered at him. 'Man don't lose well.' It came out colder than Banner would have liked, but as far as he knew it was the God's honest. He suspected more, but it wasn't the time or place for it.

'He draw on you?' The marshal ducked his chin at the dead man.

Banner nodded. 'Ask the rest. He got off the first shot.'

The marshal turned to the barkeep, then looked at the doves and cowhands crowding the saloon. 'That true?'

No one answered. Most stared and a few even went back to their card games. The doves began to drift towards the arms of winners. The noise rose again in earnest.

The marshal shook his head and blew out a deep sigh. 'Reckon it is,' he muttered and Banner knew the man wasn't going to pursue the matter. He had gotten to know the marshal in the last few days since he had arrived in Bellstar, found him affable and friendly and fair, a man who did as much as he could to administer law in a town that was as peculiar as any Banner had ridden into. Folks didn't cotton to strangers; fact, few had said a word to him since his arrival. The marshal, who hailed from a town nearly a hundred miles away, had taken over for a relative killed in the line of duty three years ago.

Banner had noticed the cold manner of the townsfolk immediately, which struck him downright odd, since one of them – he didn't know who quite yet – had summoned him here just as he finished up a case for the Forester Cattleman Association down Texas way. It puzzled him, though certainly not enough to keep him out of the local saloon. The barkeep, while untalkative, had not hesitated to keep him supplied with rotgut, though double eagles certainly helped.

The marshal eyed the 'keep. 'You get the undertaker over here and see to it this fella gets buried.'

The bartender nodded, but looked none too happy with the task.

Marshal Hart nudged his head at Banner. 'You come with me.'

Banner nodded and, locating his hat, which lay on the floor, followed the marshal to his office.

The waning afternoon sunlight stung his eyes and it almost made him regret he had decided on an early start to drinking himself into forgetfulness. The slight coolness and fresh scent to the air was a welcome relief after the stuffy, smoke and sour-booze stinking atmosphere of the saloon, though.

Reaching the marshal's office, Hart gestured for Banner to go in first.

Shutting the door behind them, the lawdog indicated a hardbacked chair and Banner felt only too eager to accept the invitation. He felt weary clear to the bone, a bit shaky from the after-effects of the whiskey and encounter in the saloon.

'That gonna be a problem?' With a nudge of his head the marshal indicated Banner's wound. 'I could fetch the doc.'

Banner glanced at his biceps. 'Scratch. I'll take whiskey to it later.'

'Suit yourself.'

'Who was he?' A coldness laced Banner's tone.

Marshal Hart glanced at Banner, then went to a small table and poured coffee from a blue enameled pot into a tin cup. 'Jack Trombley . . . but you knew that, I reckon.'

Banner ran a hand over his chin. The lines of his face deepened. 'Reckon I want to know who he was really.'

'Look like you could use this.' The marshal handed Banner the tin cup.

'Obliged.' Banner swallowed a gulp of the brew, which was cold and strong enough to clean the rust off an iron pipe. 'Judas Priest, Marshal, who taught you how to make coffee?' Banner's tone came with a touch of light-heartedness but still sapped of any warmth. Something about killing a man squeezed the heat from his soul, like night coming to a desert.

The marshal chuckled and collapsed into the chair behind his desk. He tossed his hat on the desktop and ran a finger over his iron-grey handlebar mustache.

'Reckon you need it strong, Banner. Clears out the cobwebs.'

Banner knew the man was right and that his condition was all too obvious. He had enough rotgut on his breath to singe eyebrows, but his tolerance for snake whiskey had increased in spades since the last time he tried to drown Jamie's memory, stop the nightmares from coming.

Banner frowned and eyed the lawman. 'Town ain't so helpful, Marshal. They could have backed me up.'

The marshal nodded. 'Bellstar ain't known for its hospitality and it ain't partial to strangers, not since the Culverins blasted through years back. They damn near destroyed this town and it's never rightly recovered. Now they got a gunfighter in their midst. . . .' He nudged his head at Banner and the manhunter felt a stitch of guilt mixed with a heady measure of shame in his belly.

Why don't you just call it way it is, Marshal – a killer, no better than that gang of outlaws that Donovan fella brought down a while back. Killer pure and simple.

'Reckon gunfighter ain't the proper word, Marshal,' Banner said with a prickle of irritation, despite the plain fact the lawdog was right.

The marshal nodded. 'Maybe not, but that's how they see it. You got a gun on your hip and more notches than the Culverins ever had.'

The irritation got a notch stronger. 'Culverins were vicious outlaws. I equalize their breed.'

Killer. . . .

Marshal Hart let out a humorless chuckle. 'Reckon so, and the West needs men like you, though I can't say I approve much.'

'You don't have to. It just is and will be until things change.'

The marshal twisted the tip of his mustache. 'Things are changing, Banner. West is taming in some ways. Just a matter of time till your breed dies out.'

Banner nodded, though unconvinced. If it were changing men like Trombley wouldn't be lying dead as a fence post in the back of an undertaker's wagon. 'Till it does, reckon I'm here.'

The lawdog's face turned more serious, and Banner saw a strange compassion there, something about the inner man that set him apart from many of the tin wearers he'd crossed trails with. 'There are other things that are just a matter of time, Banner. Change is just one of 'em.'

'Don't rightly catch your meaning.' Banner got a notion he did and it brought an unsettled feeling to his being.

'Death, Banner. Death is just a matter of time. For *everyone*. Men like Trombley might court it and the world won't miss their type by a damn sight, but some other folks do too. . . .'

Banner gave a somber nod. The marshal was right and maybe for a man named Luke Banner death was more than a mere matter of time; death was a bastard twin, a dark companion relentlessly following, stalking, waiting for the inevitable mistake that would let it claim its due.

The manhunter sighed and took another sip of the gunpowder coffee. The bitter liquid settled in his belly as well as the turn in conversation. 'Meanin' me?'

'Way I see it. You keep drinkin' that way and the next Trombley will plant you.' The marshal's gaze narrowed, drilling Banner, but the compassion remained. His tone lowered. 'Or maybe that's what you really want. . . .'

Banner felt a chill chase something invisible down

his spine. His gaze swept from the marshal and around the small office with its sparse furnishings of a table and coffee-pot, gun-rack with scatter-guns, a bank of three cells in the back. His unease increased. The man had likely hit the nail on the head and that made Banner no more confident the next challenge wouldn't bring him down, or that he might coddle the overwhelming urge to let it.

'You still didn't answer my question,' he said, changing the subject, though unable to chase the dark feeling out of his soul.

The marshal shrugged and his mouth settled into an expression of acceptance. 'Have it your way, Banner.' He ran a hand through his thinning hair then added: 'He rode into town a week ago or so. Reckon I don't know much about him other than the fact he appeared to be a tinhorn and a lousy one at that.'

'He was no gambler.' Banner's voice came icy and certain.

The marshal's brow crinkled. 'Don't getcha.'

'He was no gambler, just passed himself off as one.'

Marshal Hart nodded. 'Why you think that?'

Banner shrugged. 'I know men. I have to to stay alive in this business and I saw it right before . . . before he drew. He wanted that fight and I reckon he lost on purpose to create it.'

The marshal leaned back, a puzzled look drifting into his eyes. 'Again I find myself askin' why? Ain't many a man who'd reckon they could take on Luke Banner and live to tell of it.'

Banner let out a humorless laugh. 'You'd be surprised, Marshal. Ain't a week that goes by some damned fool don't take a notion to test my reputation.'

'Reckon I see that. Same thing happened with Hardin and enough others.'

The remark stung. Banner had no desire to be compared with the likes of John Wesley Hardin, a vicious hardcase. 'Hardin's a scalawag, Marshal . . .' was all he said, feeling himself bristle, though he couldn't rightly blame the marshal. Hell, maybe a killer was a killer no matter how it squared up, on the side of right or on the side of wrong.

'No offense meant, Banner. Jest that, well, you got a tendency to make bodies wherever you go and they ain't always clean ones.'

'Clean ones?'

'Ones that got a concrete reason for being dead. There's always some small doubt attached to them, 'cept maybe that killer in Texas you jest he'ped out with. It happened again tonight. I don't really like it but I can read men, too, have to be able to in this town. I think you're tellin' the truth, but if it keeps happenin' other folks won't see it that way, 'specially after what the Culverins did. You could be in for a rough time. Maybe tonight was part of that.'

Banner arched an eyebrow. 'You askin' me to get out of town?'

The marshal's face softened. 'Naw, just watch your back.'

'Always do.' Banner let a cold smile filter onto his lips.

'Do you?'

You got a death wish. . . .

Banner knew what the man was getting at and damned if he weren't inclined to agree. Many a time the dark desire to just let a bullet find him and end his turmoil nearly overcame him. But not completely, and he wondered if that weren't the Devil laughing at him.

Banner's gaze lifted to the dusty window and he stared out at the dying day. His mind drifted for long moments, and he swore he saw her standing there across the street on the boardwalk, blonde hair glistening golden in the withering sunlight, a parasol arched daintily across her shoulder.

Jamie. . . .

(Be careful, my darling. It's not your time. . . .)

A chill shuddered through him. Had she spoken? Was she truly there? Sorrow burned in his heart and his breath clutched in his throat.

Then she was gone. Her image dissolved in his memory and the boardwalk was as empty as his soul since she died.

'Banner?'

The marshal's voice prodded him from his reverie and he stared unseeing at the man a moment before his gaze focused.

'What's eatin' you, Banner? You look a hunnert miles from here and it ain't the whiskey. Your face just went three shades lighter than cow's milk.'

Banner shrugged, getting himself under control. How could he tell the marshal that he saw her more often now, especially since the last case after he watched Jim Silverbird and Shania Forester marry so happily, embrace the life he wanted so desperately with Jamie at one time? He carried no animosity towards them, not in the least, simply an envy and a mourning for things never had and lost all the same. Now her ghost was everywhere, in every bottle of rotgut and in every nightmare and sunlit corner of the day. He couldn't escape it, couldn't kill enough men to wipe it away. But he wouldn't tell Hart that, no, never. It was his ghost, his heartache, and it was the only thing he reckoned he had left that couldn't be taken from him.

When Banner didn't answer, the marshal sighed

and slapped a hand atop his desk. 'Why you here in Bellstar, Banner? Men like you don't ride into town without a damn good reason and I got a feelin' Trombley was somehow a part of it.'

Banner shrugged, thankful to be off the subject. He recollected the telegram forwarded to him from his agency, requesting his presence in Bellstar Colorado by parties unknown. Under most circumstances he would have ignored it, but after the Forester case it seemed like as good a way as any to chase the demons and ghosts away.

'You know as much as I do, Marshal. Telegram asked me to come and didn't say why. Been here three days and made myself plain but no one has approached me with the answer.'

'I don't like it, Banner. I don't like it one bit. In Bellstar it's damned unlikely anyone would go out of his way to hire a . . .'

'Killer? That what you wanted to say, Marshal?' Banner laughed, but the sound carried no emotion. 'Might as well, 'cause you're right, that's what I am. 'Nough pulp novels labeling me as such.'

'Manhunter was what I was goin' to say.' The marshal's face darkened again. 'Somethin' fishy about it. You know it, too. First I thought it might have some connection to the Red Widow Gang that's hit a few towns north and south of here, like maybe someone was gettin' nervous Bellstar would be next. But I don't reckon that's it for some reason.'

Banner nodded. 'Got me that notion, too. They've avoided Bellstar for some reason. 'Course there ain't a hell of a lot here to hit since the Culverins came through. Folks have made sure of that. Just the occasional stage headed from the mines going south. Lot richer towns to try for.'

'Reckon you're right, but someone wanted you here for a reason.'

Banner gave another nod. 'Reckon I just gotta wait it out.'

'Someone might be settin' you up, Banner. That fella tonight. . . .'

Banner was inclined to agree. Trombley had forced that fight and there had to be a reason. But was it connected to his being called here? Maybe a loose end somewhere had come back to haunt him.

'Got me enough enemies. Maybe one of 'em took a notion to get even.'

The marshal gave a scoffing laugh. 'Thought you didn't leave none of 'em alive?'

Banner felt the remark cut, but let it go. 'Got enough I don't even know about, Marshal. Any damn fool with a chip on his shoulder might take a notion to test his mettle and earn himself a reputation by bringing down a famous manhunter. Damn pulp writers just made that all the worse. Maybe that's all that happened tonight.'

'Maybe, but somehow I doubt that's the end of it.'

A dark feeling wandered over Banner. Somewhere deep inside his revenge-driven soul he knew the man was right. It would not end at the saloon and in fact it might not end until he was the one lying in blood with a killer's bullet buried in his heart. . . .

Shadows gathered in a far corner of the saloon, bunching around a door that led to a back hallway and storage rooms. The first touches of dusk had invaded the establishment and low-turned lanterns cast buttery light that mixed with the thick haze of Durham smoke and shafts of fading daylight filtering in through the dusty windows. The activities had resumed in earnest, despite the earlier gunfight. Whiskey went down in copious amounts and in some cases came up the same way as some cowhand misjudged his limit and made use of the clumped sawdust on the floor. Laughter and shouts and giggles punctuated the atmosphere, stabbing above the discordant jangle of the plinkety piano.

Hell of a thing, thought the man in the low-pulled Stetson, who stood with his back against the wall near that back door. Not more than twenty minutes ago Jack Trombley had been dragged out by his boots by the 'taker and hoisted into the back of a wagon and not a gawdamned soul seemed to recollect it. Hell, the blood hadn't even been scrubbed from the floor; damn 'keep had just tossed a handful of new sawdust over it.

Well, hell, it made no nevermind, did it? No one would miss Jack Trombley and rightly so. He was a sonofabitch.

The door was open a crack and he glanced towards it, but quickly jerked his gaze away. Some things didn't need to have a face put to them and he reckoned what lay behind that door was one of them.

Nerves dancing four-four in a three-quarter waltz, his gaze skipped around the room, to the various cowhands and tinhorns hunched over tables, involved in poker games, chuck-a-luck and bucking the tiger, then to the bar doves, their creamy bosoms displayed to near peak before winners' lusty gazes. He shot a glance at the piano player banging away at the ivories without so much as a notion of tune.

The man's nerves tightened further as at last his sight settled on the place where his partner had met death at the hands of Luke Banner. Gawdamn, it shouldn't have turned out that way, not at all. Trombley had the jump on Banner and Banner had been drunk. It should have been so easy, cut and dried and money collected. But Banner walked away scot free and the man took a notion there was a lick more to the manhunter than he or Trombley had thought. Damn them pulp writers and their factless imaginations, though by damn maybe what they said was true this one time. Maybe Banner was hell on a horse and had killed all those men.

The man gave violent shudder and shook his head, struggling to force the thoughts from his mind. It would do him no good to get the rabbit about him, not now, not after what he'd been hired to do and not with who had hired him. That was worse than Banner, and if he didn't follow through with this job he would be the next stiffening corpse in the back of that wagon. Banner was the lesser of two evils, though the man cursed himself for ever getting the gawdamn fool notion to take this job and join up with. . . .

Hell's bells! He couldn't even think that name! It wasn't safe, not in these parts and not if he wanted to live out his years. Best just accept that and belly up to it.

He couldn't stand the crawling sensation in his hide any longer and tilted his head towards the door opening, knowing someone would be waiting within the darkness of that back hall.

'You there?' he asked in a harsh whisper.

'You're late!' came a voice from behind the door, low and husky, as if whoever it was was speaking through a bandanna and purposely disguising the tone. One thing was plain, though, a good deal of venom dressed the voice.

'Had us a bit of difficulty. . . .' The man felt his jitters worsen and tensed for the reply.

'Trombley failed. . . .'

The man nodded. 'He's dead. Banner got the jump on him.'

A curse came from behind the door. 'Banner wasn't drunk enough.'

The man let out a scoffing laugh. 'You sure he ever would be? He's got goddamn lightnin' in his hand. And he hits what he aims for.'

A laugh sounded, and still the man, whose name was Henkins, couldn't tell anything about the person behind the voice. Fact was, he damn well didn't want to know because it would mean instant death. 'Men like that have too much guilt to be sober too long. Banner's no different. Except his guilt will be relieved very soon – if I have to kill him myself.'

'Not so sure of that,' Henkins muttered, doubt crawling through him. He wasn't afeared of many men, but Banner. . . .

'Don't get a notion to back out, Henkins. It ain't an option.'

Henkins shuddered, the threat plain. 'No, reckon it ain't.'

'Man across the street on the corner named Zurk. Go meet him. He knows you're comin'.'

'What are we s'posed to do?' The fear bled into his voice, now, and he got the sinking feeling he wouldn't like what was coming.

'You're gettin' another chance at Banner. . . .'

Henkins' belly dropped, but there was no refusing. With Banner he stood a chance; with what lay behind that door he had none. His hand slid over his gun butt, but it provided him no comfort. He whispered a prayer to a God he hadn't spoken to in the years since he had killed his first man, knowing it would do no good. God didn't listen to killers and rightly so. But he prayed it anyway.

Prayed it wasn't a good day to discover hell and damnation wasn't just a story told by Sunday morning preachers and the Devil wasn't a goat-headed monster laying claim to his blackened soul.

TWO

Banner stepped out of the marshal's office into the deepening dusk, a heaviness crushing his soul. A man had died tonight, by his hand, when he could have prevented it. But he hadn't prevented it. He had hastened it, let the dark entity of vengeance inside him win.

It won't end till lead finds you. . . .

Was that true? Was there no other way out? He pondered that more and more these days.

He had gotten lucky in the saloon. Rotgut had slowed his reflexes more than they had deteriorated already, stolen his balance, but, for some reason known only to his Maker, not his accuracy. Or was that dumb luck?

Maybe a bit of both. Whatever it was, he should by all rights have been the one lying dead in the sawdust, memories scattered around him in each drop of blood spilled. Memories and regrets, too goddamn many to count or care about any more.

But you do care, Banner. And that's what haunts you. . . .

A twinge of remorse twisted in his belly as the image of the dead man invaded his mind. Another ghost.

He drew a deep breath, the scent of dust and manure assailing his nostrils. He eyed the wide main street of the Colorado town, gaze sweeping from the livery to the saloon, the mercantile's to the lawyer's, the general store to the blacksmith's. Bellstar looked peaceful now, belying the deed done earlier, its false-front buildings bearing no witness yet still eerily somber, damning. Folks sauntered along the boardwalk, but not a passer-by cast him a straight look. A few times he caught folks glancing surreptitiously from the corners of their eyes, faces twisted with disapproval.

They had reacted that way since the day he rode in. The marshal attributed it to the legacy of the outlaw band who once destroyed this town and perhaps that was the case. Perhaps the Peacemaker resting in the worn holster thonged to his thigh made that all the more likely, though he rightly didn't give a damn. The only thing he cared about was he had been called here to do a job and three days into his stay no one had approached him with so much as hi-di-ho and that puzzled him.

He had reread the telegram numerous times, contacted his agency for more information, yet beyond the fact that the missive had been sent from Bellstar there was little else. His first stop – well, after the livery and half a bottle of rotgut in the saloon – had been the telegraph office where he'd had a parley with the operator, who was as forthcoming as most in this town. So far he was looking at a solid nothing and feeling more than a little antsy about it. Usually the folks who hired him met him straight out, asked him to do a deed that would not stain their own hands. Yet it did, it soiled theirs as much as it did his; they just didn't know it. A killing ordered – even a legitimate one – still took a piece off a man's soul.

Banner reckoned he had damn few pieces left.

He walked along the boardwalk, boots cropping hollowly on the dusty boards. Shadows lengthened, creeping from corners and alleys like living things as the setting sun slid behind the distant blue peaks of the Rockies.

Next time you won't be so lucky. Next time might be the last time. Is that what you want?

Maybe it was. Maybe it had all caught up with him. He felt so ... *worn*, leaden in his soul and Jamie's memory waited for him at every turn. He wanted to be with her, stop this infernal desire to kill, send the dark thing inside him back to hell where it belonged.

You had your chance. You could have let Trombley kill you.

He reckoned that was right, but when it came down to it maybe something inside struggled to live, struggled to somehow find that last shred of human decency and hope, that lost dream. But that something was tainted and locked in a desperate battle, one it likely couldn't win. He knew the marshal was right: it was just a matter of time. He had slipped, maybe too much. It happened to gunfighters, the slowing reflexes, the stiffness that crept into a man's fingers each morning, the eyes that lost their sharpness just enough to make a body hesitate. And die.

Banner shook his head and forced his brooding thoughts away. It didn't matter a lick, now, did it? Because whoever had called him here, for whatever reason, might have just sent a welcoming card in the form of a dead tinhorn earlier this afternoon. And now Banner had to watch his back – or end up flat on it.

A sudden quiver of apprehension coursing through him, his gaze jumped to the building tops.

What was it?

Something. . . .

Gaze sweeping from rooftop to rooftop, he hoped to catch a glint of dying sunlight on gun metal, but saw nothing to explain the feeling dogging him. Yet something felt distinctly wrong. That sixth sense he had honed to such a fine edge over the years of chasing down hardcases was warning him. A quiver of danger, of threat. At least that hadn't dulled – as long as he was sober, he amended, and at the moment he was acutely so.

Where did the threat come from?

His gaze traveled downward, to the boardwalk and alleys, beneath buckboards. He peered at each trough and barrel for any sign of movement, menace. . . .

A scream jolted him and he tensed, hand slapping to his gun butt, but not drawing. A woman's scream, coming from just up the street to the left.

His gaze jerked in that direction; folks on the street and boardwalk suddenly shuffled off in the opposite direction.

Without thought or hesitation Banner was in motion, pressing close to buildings as he made his way along the boardwalk, taking care to make as little noise with his boots as possible. His heart beat thickly and his face went grim.

An alley lay just ahead and he paused, hearing the sounds of a scuffle coming from within. He knew now why he had felt that sense of danger, though usually it warned him when he was the target, not someone else.

He would have time to think on that later. The scream had brought a note of mortal terror and that needed his full attention. If he blundered into the situation he *would* be the target and one near miss in an afternoon was quite enough.

His breath quickened and the thing inside him stirred.

You feel it, Banner, that itch to kill, to punish. You remember her dying scream. . . .

Another shriek, this one snapped short, then muffled sounds and a string of curses from another voice.

He edged forward, reaching the alley and pausing. He eased around the corner, hand ready to go for the Peacemaker.

His gaze took in the scene immediately, spotting two men, one holding onto a woman from behind, hand clasped over her mouth. A hardcase, instantly recognizable as such.

The other man stood in front of the woman, slightly to the left, a Bowie knife in one hand tasting the air before him, her handbag clutched in the other. The woman was struggling furiously and Banner saw scratch marks and blood dribbling down the knife-wielder's face. The sleeve of her blue hip-length jacket was torn.

She suddenly lashed a vicious backward kick, raking the man's shin for probably not the first time and the man nearly lost his hold. She tried to jerk free but he managed to hold on.

'Kill her, for Chrissakes!' he bellowed to his partner, whose face twisted with a malicious look.

Banner lunged as the man's knife started forward. The distance was only a matter of few yards and he had little choice if he were going to prevent her from being skewered.

The man holding the woman saw Banner coming and bellowed a warning to his companion.

The hardcase with the knife spun and Banner got the sudden notion he had been expected, that somehow the man had been waiting for his lunge and was ready to counter it. The hardcase swung the Bowie knife around to meet Banner's attack, slashing wildly.

Banner twisted with better balance than he had exhibited in the saloon and the blade sailed past him, just missing his side. He pivoted and brought a fist up in a short powerful uppercut.

A *crack*! like blocks colliding sounded and the bandit's eyes seemed to search the inside of his head then settle back. His eyelids fluttered and he staggered backwards a few steps, but maintained his grip on the knife.

The woman managed to bite the hand of the hardcase holding her and as he jerked his bleeding palm away she let out a shriek.

The hardcase swung her around violently and hurled her towards the wall. She hit hard, air exploding from her lungs and the boards shuddered. Her face went blank and she slid down, stunned.

Banner's blood boiled but he got little time to think about it.

The hardcase with the knife recovered, charged. The other outlaw rushed him from the side.

Banner tried to sidestep, grab an arm of one bandit and send him sailing into the other, but the move was slightly mistimed and he missed the knife arm. The maneuver was enough to keep him from getting stuck though the blade slit the side of his denim shirt.

The man's arm, driven by momentum, kept going and Banner cradled it, twisting. A snap sounded and the man bleated. The knife dropped to the dust.

The second man slammed into Banner then. The manhunter, occupied with the knife-wielder, had lost sight of him.

A punch took him square in the side of the head and his senses danced. He let go of the knife-wielding hardcase and stumbled backwards, the alley gyrating before him. He crashed into the wall and the impact snapped his senses clear.

The second hardcase was charging him again, fist hungry for the finishing blow.

Banner jerked his head left and the punch slammed into the wall with a bang as loud as a gunshot. The manhunter launched another uppercut and it took the man under his jaw, nearly lifting him off the ground and sending him staggering backward, arms wind-milling. The hardcase kept going until he collided with the opposite wall, a glazed look in his eyes.

The knife-wielder, gripping his broken arm, bolted for the other end of the alley. He had had his fill of the manhunter and was counting his losses, even if it meant leaving his partner to the wolves.

The second man hardly cottoned to the idea and stumbled for the front of the alley, rounding the corner. Banner heard his boots clomping along the boardwalk.

He took half a notion to chase them down, but gave it up as his gaze settled on the woman. They were likely just a couple of run-of-the-mill hardcases who would look for easier pickings in the future.

Were they run-of-the-mill? Or was there more to this than it appeared?

The notion crossed his mind, along with the thought that they had been expecting him, but he shook his head, dismissing it as a manhunter on the sundown side getting a little more paranoid than he should.

He went to the woman, and scooched, eyeing her. Her face carried couple of ripening bruises and small scrapes, but she looked little damaged beyond that. She gazed at him, blue eyes finding his, dazed but coming back and something inside him froze.

For the briefest of moments he saw her there, his

Jamie, staring back at him from a memory. A shiver of sadness took his heart and his breath clutched.

Then Jamie's face dissolved and he saw the woman clearly. Not Jamie, no, never Jamie. Jamie was gone. Forever. This woman was beautiful if bruised and reminded him of the woman he had loved, but was not her.

'You all right, ma'am?' His voice came shakier than he would have liked. Her sapphire eyes locked with his and for a moment he felt as if she were searching him, perhaps trying to ascertain whether he intended her harm. The expression quickly vanished and she tried to smile, but it was strained.

Banner straightened and helped her to her feet. She appeared unsteady a moment, then smoothed out her jacket by tugging on its bottom. She was wearing a walking-out dress, V-shaped *décolletage* filled in with a frilled lace collar, which was now soiled and torn. Her sleeves were elbow-length with turned-back cuffs and lace ruffles. Her double skirt flared from her old fashioned curved hips, overskirt turned back to reveal the silk lining. Her laced high shoes were scuffed and dust coated.

'Much obliged, gent,' Her voice sent a shiver through his being. It was like Jamie's, soft, mellifluous, laced with the promise of feminine delights and soft whispers and it stirred the ghosts inside him.

Words locking in his throat, Banner nodded and stepped back. He retrieved her handbag, which the hardcase had dropped in the dust when Banner hit him, and kicked the Bowie knife away. He handed her the bag and, taking her elbow, guided her out to the boardwalk. A few passers-by ignored them, appearing skittish. He gazed down the street, seeing no sign of the hardcases.

Removing his bandanna he went to the trough and dipped it in the water, then went back to the woman, who, weakened from her ordeal, was leaning against the rail. He dabbed at the spots of blood around her lip and daubed off the smudges of dirt on her cheek, then stuffed the bandanna into his pocket. She was entirely beautiful, from her blonde pinned-back hair, its tiny curls framing her high forehead, to the slight upturn of her nose. Small lines shown around her eyes and lips, but they only enhanced her beauty, maturing it and evoking a distant longing in Banner's soul. Her jacket stretched taut across her ripe bosom and he forced himself to avert his gaze, suddenly uneasy.

She gazed at his arm, then back up. 'You've been hurt, too . . .'

He gave an easy laugh. 'Reckon I'll live, ma'am, but you look like you could use a cup of tea or something a mite stronger?'

She gave a small smile and a shudder suddenly went through her. Her eyes glossed with tears and Banner prayed she wouldn't cry. He didn't think he could stand that. He felt awkward as hell as it was. She appeared to recover from her spell and though he reckoned he couldn't blame her after what she had been through, he couldn't deny he felt relieved, either.

'Reckon that 'd be a bit of heaven, Mr. . . ?'

'Banner, Luke Banner.'

She curtsied and her smile widened, warmed. 'I'm Cynthia Addleson, Mr Banner. Pleased to make your acquaintance.'

He guided her into the small eatery two blocks down and they settled at a corner table. The room was rife with the scents of fresh sourdough biscuits and strong coffee, peach pie, beefsteak. Hanging lanterns blended with dying daylight to give the place with its fifteen tables covered with blue-checked cloths a comfortable atmosphere. He remained silent until their order arrived, fighting to keep his gaze from lingering on the woman before him. He had to admit her resemblance to Jamie did things to him, things he wanted to deny existed within a man named Luke Banner. She sipped a cup of jasmine tea – Banner reckoned the eatery's owner had spent time traveling in the Orient – and he took a drink of Arbuckle's, which was considerably milder than the marshal's version.

'You new here in Bellstar?' he asked finally, gaze locking with hers.

She tilted her head coquettishly. 'Why, yes, how did you know?'

He shrugged. 'Most folks here ain't the friendly sort. You're not like them. Reckon this ain't quite the reception you expected, though.'

She gave him a small laugh, but a note of fear underlaid it. 'Reckon not. Well, you are right, Mr Banner. I just arrived yesterday, on the stage. I'm traveling from Wyoming way to meet my sister's family down in New Mex.'

Banner nodded. 'Best be on your way, then, as soon as possible. Bellstar ain't as safe as it could be.' His tone carried more sarcasm than he intended and he wondered if there weren't a trace of a lie, too. Did he want Cynthia Addleson to be on her way so soon? At all?

'I'm here for a week, Mr Banner, until the next passenger stage comes through. It was quite against my wishes, let me assure you, but I will make the best of it.' Her eyes softened, reached into his in a flirtatious manner that reminded him of the way Jamie used to playfully tease him. He wondered if he could feel any more uneasily comfortable. She gave an easy laugh. 'I won't be attending to another telegram, let me tell you that.' She took a sip of tea, blue eyes holding his as she did so.

Jamie. . . .

'Telegram?' A note of apprehension went through Banner. He couldn't put a finger on it, but he got the impression he was about to become more puzzled.

'Why, yes, the hotel man delivered a note to me. Told me to come to the telegraph office to retrieve a missive from my sister.'

Something about that struck Banner as suspicious. 'Why didn't the hotel man just give you the telegram?'

Her eyes took on a look of surprise. 'Why, you're right, Mr Banner. I reckon I didn't think of that. I just thought my sister wouldn't send a telegram unless it was very important and I must see to it. Curious thing is, when I got to the telegraph office there was nothing waiting for me. The operator seemed to have no idea what I was talking about. I will be sure to ask the hotel man about it when I go back, let me tell you.'

The revelation didn't surprise Banner a lick and warning bells were clanging in his mind. The impression he had taken of being waited for in that alley got stronger. Not just waited for, but *lured*, and whoever had done it had used Cynthia Addleson as the perfect bait.

He sighed and leaned back in his chair, the lines in his brow deepening. 'Those men in the alley, you ever see either of 'em before?'

She gave a slight shake of her head. 'Why, no, never, Mr Banner. I expect they just wanted my handbag, which God's honest had nothing of value in it other than a few pieces of silver. I left most my money in the hotel safe.'

Banner nodded. He studied the woman and decided

she was telling the truth. He wondered if she had been made an unwitting pawn in a bigger scheme to get at him, but that left too many unanswered questions in his mind. Whoever had sent her the note had timed it too perfectly, which might mean someone was watching him, had known he was with the marshal, perhaps had seen the killing in the saloon. Arranged a second attempt on his life.

Are you getting loco? Looking for killers around every corner? Have the years of killing and countless enemies caught up with you?

He wondered. Was he manufacturing links where none existed? Whatever the case, the mystery had deepened and now he felt positive someone had lured him to Bellstar for some reason other than a job, perhaps to even kill him. But who? And why?

'Penny for your thoughts, Mr Banner?'

His gaze focused back on Cynthia, who was peering at him with slight concern. He smiled. 'Just thinkin' 'bout them men, ma'am. Likely you just happened to be in the wrong place at the wrong time but I wouldn't take any chances. You best stay in your hotel as much as possible till that stage comes.'

She laughed and it carried a note of mocking that puzzled him.

'I assure you, Mr Banner I am not one to turn tail and hide. Those men might have frightened me some but I assure you at least one of them will have more bruises than I do.'

Banner chuckled and reckoned he had mistaken mockery for feistiness. Cynthia Addleson was no school marm and that was a trait that reminded him even more of Jamie. 'Those men might have killed you, ma'am.'

She smiled. 'But they didn't and I reckon I am most

fortunate you came along, Mr Banner. But if you are worried, I would be much obliged if you would see me back to my hotel.' She gave him a coy smile that sent a shiver through his soul.

Before he could stop himself he said, 'Reckon I'd like that just fine, ma'am.'

She'll die, just like Jamie. . . .

He should have felt a certain sense of prospect and providence then, but he did not. Instead he felt the darkness inside him strengthen, stirred by a brooding sense of fate and dice cast that always rolled up snake eyes. And as he guided her out of the eatery Luke Banner wondered if he hadn't just taken another step towards his own personal hell.

THREE

Henkins and Zurk, the knife-wielding hardcase, stood in an alley near the saloon. Darkness had fallen and the night was marbled with shadow and the glow of the half moon. The chilly spring air made Henkins's breath steam out. Despite the briskness, trickles of sweat zigzagged down his face. His gaze darted about, as if searching for a threat in every direction, which in fact he was. They had failed. For the second time in a few hours Banner had walked away scot free and that wouldn't sit well with his employer. Not well at all.

The image of Trombley's dead staring face invaded his mind and for the second time in more years than he could recollect he uttered a prayer that he'd live out the night. He cursed himself for getting into something like this, but how was he to know? When he accepted the invitation scribbled on the back of a business card to meet this mysterious employer at the back of the saloon he half thought it was a joke. But it was no joke. He had never been allowed to see who he was talking to, only knew the five double eagles in a small parfleche tossed at his feet was more than he could make in months hiring out to local spreads. Greed and gold had curtailed any sense of curiosity and apprehension he should have felt and now it was too late.

'What the hell's takin' so long?' his partner blurted, a jitter in his voice. Henkins looked over and saw the sudden flare of a lucifer flash piss-colored light across the man's worried features. A cheroot glowed to life and the match blinked out.

Henkins shrugged. 'Dunno. Card said to meet here at eight. Reckon it ain't much past that.'

Zurk grunted. 'Feels like it, that's shore as hell.' The cigarette's red tip bobbed as he spoke. 'I don't like it a lick. Got me a notion to just pull stakes—'

'Put that out, you fool!' a voice snapped from behind them and to the left. Henkins jolted and looked in that direction, but saw only a vague shadowy form outlined near the wall.

'Christamighty, you scared the bejesus outta us!' Zurk blurted and the red tip twirled to the ground like a dying firefly. He stamped it out and the alley seemed suddenly darker, colder, more threatening.

'You missed Banner. . . .' The voice, low and muffled, came with gunpowder accusation and Henkins shuddered. The figure took a step forward and the hardcase caught a flash of red clothing in a wedge of moonlight. The face appeared to be covered by some dark cloth, the figure loosely dressed. Then the figure moved into shadow and though the hardcase squinted he saw nothing.

'Best not get too curious, Henkins,' the figure said and Henkins realized he'd been caught staring. He jerked his gaze away. 'Ain't healthy.'

'We tried.' Zurk's voice had lost any inflection of bravado. 'Banner's tougher than you think.'

A mocking laugh echoed through the darkness, embedding itself in Henkins's soul. 'I know more about him than you'll ever know. . . .' A swish of clothing sounded and the sudden percussion of a shot thundered through the alley. A flash of flame splashed orange-yellow light across the figure, showing a glimpse of red and black.

Zurk skipped backwards and slammed into the building wall, hanging there a moment. Another shot; the sound of lead punching into muscle and bone and he crumpled to the alley floor.

Henkins's mouth dropped in shock. He stared at the shadowed body, hearing a gurgle as blood pumped from a hole in the man's chest.

'W-why'd you kill him?' he stammered, terrified his question would be answered by another shot and he would feel the burning punch of lead boring into his body.

'The answer's obvious: he failed. He was s'posed to kill Banner. You were s'posed to hold the girl.'

'Christamighty, Banner's not so easy to kill!'

'All men are easy to kill, Henkins. You just gotta do it right. Ask your friend. . . .'

Heavy silence filled the alley and Henkins heard his heart thumping against his ribs and his pulse throbbing in his veins. 'You . . . you ain't gonna kill me?'

A laugh gave him another shudder. 'I damn well should, but you got another chance. You'll ride with us on the next job.'

'What about Banner?' He couldn't hide the relief that surged in his voice, though it came mixed with a feeling of doom at the prospect of what lay ahead.

'Leave him be for the time being. Don't show yourself around, neither. I don't want him recognizing you and following you back to me somehow. He's no goddamn fool. He wouldn't have lived this long if'n he were. When I need you you'll find a card at your door.'

'What about that girl? You still want her roughed up?'

A pause; it gave Henkins the heebie-jeebies. Something about being in the darkness with this figure, one who killed without remorse and without warning made him wish he could just ride out and never turn back, forget all about Colorado and Luke Banner.

'She's no use to us, now. Let her be. I just needed bait to lure Banner into that alley and weren't no other strangers in town.'

'How'd you get her on the street when you needed it?'

An angry grunt came from the shadows. 'You ask too goddamn many questions and you'll be worm food with your partner.'

'Didn't mean nothin',' Henkins mumbled, knowing he'd damn well better not push his luck. Relief flooded him at being rid of the job of killing Banner, but he wondered if what the figure said about riding with the rest would be worse.

Henkins glanced up and stared into the shadows and surprise hit his features, along with another surge of relief. The figure was gone, like a ghost fading with the morning light. He glanced at the body sprawled on the alley floor and gave a shudder, wondering just how long it would be until his blood soaked the ground.

Luke Banner stared at the amber liquid in the bottle sitting atop the small table. He sat straddling a hard-backed chair in his room at the boarding house at the edge of town. The room held sparse furnishings: a bed, a small bureau with a porcelain wash basin resting atop, a rickety wooden table, and a low-turned lantern on a nightstand. The lantern cast anemic light across blue fleur-de-lis wallpaper that peeled in as many places as it stuck. The window was cracked, part of a pane broken out and every goddamn cricket north of the Pecos seemed to be making as much noise as it could.

He grabbed the bottle and swallowed a deep drink, the liquor searing its way down his gullet; it settled like fire in his belly. His head dipped and he thought his chin would smash into the table but it was merely an illusion of his alcohol-hazed mind. He laughed, a sound that held no humor and perhaps a measure of insanity.

What's so goddamn funny, Banner? The pathetic sot you've become? The thunder of your own guilt and mule-headed sense of self-preservation? You want to go on this way? Trying to outrun her memory, the nightmares? They'll find you everywhere you go. You can't stop them because they're all you have left. You have to end it. . . .

Sweat trickled from beneath his arms and down his face. Nausea pulled at his belly and he was damned if he knew how he was managing to hold his stomach down.

She looks so much like Jamie. . . .

She did. The same blonde hair and infatuating guileless smile, the same sapphire-blue eyes and innocent laugh. A coy sense of femininity that promised a revelation of secrets to the man lucky enough to share her life.

A rush of sorrow and grief washed through him and he slammed the bottle on the table.

His meeting with Cynthia Addleson had disturbed him more than he thought, and after leaving her off at her hotel he felt overwhelmed by a haunting sense of things never had but lost all the same. He'd wandered back to his room half in a daze.

At first he struggled to push the thoughts away, though with little success. The woman was quite fetching in his estimation, but for more than just her outer beauty. She reminded him of a life that never was, a life that could have been, *should* have been, and that aroused things deep inside his soul, things the dark demon of vengeance inside him had fought to conceal all these years.

It's no use, Banner. She's not Jamie and you can't bring her back. No matter how many men you kill, no matter how many ghosts you slaughter, and Cynthia Addleson won't change that a lick. She'll be gone in a week. Let her be done with it.

Grabbing the whiskey, he swallowed another gulp then slammed the bottle back down. Goddamned if he didn't want to see her again, despite every rational voice inside telling him he was a fool.

If you can't bring Jamie back maybe . . .

NO!

What the devil was he thinking? He could not risk getting close to anyone, now, or ever, not in his line of work. Hell, two attempts on his life in a few hours should have made that plain. How could he expose Cynthia Addelson to that? Anyone he dared get close to would die. No two ways about it.

Maybe if you gave this up, took another name and just disappeared into the west. . . ?

At that thought he uttered a mushy laugh. It was almost funny, almost goddamn funny, though the notion had occurred to him more than once since seeing Jim Silverbird marry Shania Forester. What the hell would he do? Start a new life? Be a rancher way he originally planned with Jamie? Someone would find him, somehow, and it would be over, for him and for whoever he chose to love.

There might be a way. . . .

Hell there was! Even if he could ghosts would be

waiting for him every night, in every black corner of his mind, in every grief-corrupted memory.

A heavy depression washed over him and suddenly he felt crushed by the thing of vengeance he had become. He slammed a fist on the table and the bottle jumped, but remained upright. His vision blurred and when it focused again he was staring at his hands, seeing streams of blood run over them, through his fingers, dripping onto the table and puddling.

'Nooo!' he yelled, shaking his hands, trying to get the crimson liquid off and suddenly it was gone, another blood-stained memory. For a moment he thought he heard laughing, the echoes of the men he had killed.

You're a killer, Banner. Plain and simple. That's all you'll ever be. You have no other life and you're no good. You can't go on this way . . . you can't face the ghosts any more and you can't let yourself love.

No, he could not. He couldn't risk her life and he could offer her nothing except the fear that one day something from his past would catch up to them and end any happiness he dared take from life. He was dead inside, a creature of vengeance and retribution that took life and set himself up as God.

Killer.

Yes, that was what he was. Manhunter, hired gun, avenging angel – call it what you would but it all came down to the same thing:

Killer.

'Banner!'

His head jerked up and saw a man standing by the door.

'Christamighty . . .' he whispered and the ragged blood-stained hand of Jack Trombley lifted, pointing an accusing finger. A hole showed clearly in his chest and accusation glittered in his glassy eyes.

'You murdered me, Banner! You could have stopped it. You had a choice, but you did it anyway. You're a butcher, not a saint who doles out justice. You could have let me live!'

The words roared in Banner's ears and he jammed his hands against them, trying to shut out the ghost's damning accusations. He pressed his eyes shut, but still saw the man standing there, pointing at him, condemning him.

'Nooo!' he screamed. 'You're dead!'

Killer!

The room went silent, except for the hammering of his heart. Opening his eyes he stared at the door. The gambler was gone, never there in the first place, simply concocted by black memory and snake whiskey. But the damage was done.

You could have stopped it!

Banner's hand slipped over the butt of his Peacemaker and he slowly pulled it free. Placing it atop the table he stared at it. The instrument of destruction, the device of retribution. The god-maker. But, no, that wasn't quite right, was it? *He* was that device, not the Colt. He was responsible for murder. The gun was merely the lightning from the hand, a means to the end.

The end of a man who had no feelings. A man who killed other men, and smote them from the earth like that angry Biblical God.

A means to freedom? And finish to all the guilt and pain and ghosts?

Banner lifted the Colt and checked the chamber, seeing six bullets resting comfortably in their slots. He had seen to its reloading the minute he had come to his room.

You can't let it go on. . . .

Couldn't he? Was there that chance for some other life now?

He raised the gun to his temple.

Sweat streamed down his face as he felt the cool metal press into his flesh.

Pull it! Pull the trigger. End this nightmare and be with her.

His finger slid over the trigger, trembling. He took a deep breath, knowing one shot would do it, send him to hell with the men he had killed, where they could have their fill of tearing his soul to pieces and where he would be free of all pain.

Would you be free, Banner? Or would you suffer eternally, damned like the men you killed?

He didn't know. He didn't know if he believed in any goddamn Devil and Hell, only the hell he lived right now.

('Luke. . . .')

The voice came soft, from somewhere deep in his memory and his gaze flicked up. She was there again, standing before him, his Jamie, beckoning with outstretched arms.

'J-Jamie . . .' he whispered. 'I can't go on any more without you.'

('It is not your time, Luke. Not this way.')

'What way, Jamie? What way?'

The figure dissolved; emptiness seeped from the walls, his soul.

His hand trembled, palm damp and a small cry escaped his lips. He suddenly lowered the gun, slid it into its holster.

He couldn't do it.

Something inside him still wanted to go on, though damned if he knew why. Maybe it was her memory after all, the only thing he had ever been true to other than his hunger for vengeance. He didn't know. Maybe he did want to die, maybe he did court it, but not that way, a coward's way. Luke Banner was many things, not the least of them a cold-hearted bastard at times, but he was no coward.

A tear almost slid from his eye, but not quite. He reckoned there was nothing like that left inside him anymore. A knock stuttered on the door, muffled, and for a moment he wasn't even sure he had heard anything or whether it had come from his memory and stupor. He looked up at the door and the knock came again, clearer this time. He peered at it, realizing he had forgotten to lock the goddamn thing, another sign he was slipping and one he couldn't rightly afford.

His hand stayed on his Peacemaker. 'It's unlocked,' he said, voice slurred.

The door opened and Marshal Hart stepped into the room, hat in one hand, a rolled-up paper in the other. The marshal's eyes flicked from Banner to the whiskey bottle. 'Jesus H., Banner, you lookin' to drink yourself to death?'

Banner gave a humorless laugh. 'That the easiest way?'

The marshal stepped deeper into the room and studied Banner a moment. 'Was gonna ask if you'd been near the saloon in the last hour, but I reckon this answers my question.'

Banner nodded. 'Got my own stock and ain't been nowhere but with my ghosts, Marshal. Join me?' With a tilt of his head, Banner indicated the whiskey bottle.

The marshal shook his head. 'Ghosts?' He paused studying Banner. 'Yeah, reckon a man like you has plenty of 'em.'

'You come here for a reason or just to criticize my personal habits?' The words came out with more venom than he intended, but what the hell? One more enemy didn't rightly matter.

The marshal chuckled. 'Looks like I don't have to. You got enough guilt already.' The marshal stepped over to the table and tossed down the paper. It unrolled, curled at both ends, and Banner stared at it. A Wanted dodger. 'You seen this fella before?'

Banner nodded slowly. 'Reckon. Why?'

'Whore from the saloon stumbled over him in an alley a bit ago. Dead as a can of corned beef. Someone put two extra holes in his hide.'

'You figure I did it?' Banner cocked an eyebrow.

The marshal shrugged, looking slightly apologetic. 'Reckoned there was a chance.'

' 'Nother unclean body?'

The marshal nodded. 'Yep, but I got me the notion his face looked a mite familiar so I checked my dodgers and sure 'nuff there he was. Wanted for two murders as it is and maybe more that ain't known about. Usually the case with his type. World won't miss him, but I was curious. How you know him?'

Banner gave a small laugh. 'Tried to add a third body to his record earlier. Came upon him and another man in an alley. They were attacking a woman and this man' – he indicated the dodger – 'tried to gut me.'

The marshal played with the end of his mustache, a puzzled look in his eyes. 'Woman?'

'Cynthia Addleson. Stayin' at the hotel.'

'I'll check with her 'bout it, then. But can't rightly say as I give a damn. He saved me or some other lawdog the trouble of throwin' him a necktie party.'

Banner was inclined to agree. The hardcase deserved what he got, though it only served to deepen the mystery already surrounding the events that had occurred since he arrived in Bellstar. If this man had been part of a plan to kill him why had he been murdered? Because he failed?

The marshal scooped the dodger and rolled it back up. Going to the door, he stopped and drilled Banner with a serious gaze. 'What you do for a livin', Banner, I might not rightly approve of. But such as it is it is needed in these parts, least for now. Wish it weren't that way, but you got nothin' to feel guilty about.'

'Don't I?' Banner's face went dark. In his estimation he sure as hell did.

The marshal let out a small laugh. 'No more than I do, I reckon. Not as long as men like this' – he held up the dodger – 'are the ones gettin' buried.'

'You got it nice an' legal, Marshal. Badge says so.'

The marshal nodded. 'Reckon you're right, but some lawdogs like Earp and the rest ain't much better than the ones they protect us from. Just keep that in mind.'

'That s'posed to make me feel honorable?' Banner couldn't keep the sarcastic challenge from his voice.

'Ain't s'posed to make you feel anything. But it might give you a reason, leastwise better than the one you got now, if I read you right.'

Banner felt a chill somewhere inside. 'My reason might have reached its end, Marshal.'

'All things do. Maybe it's time you think about findin' somethin' else, then, 'fore the choice is made for you.'

The marshal stepped out and closed the door behind him, leaving Luke Banner alone with his ghosts and a nagging feeling the lawman was dead right.

A sudden burst of anger raged through him and his arm swept out, sending the whiskey bottle flying from the table. For long moments he gave in to the feeling, letting the fury course through his veins. Then a cold sense of numbness took over, mixing with drunken-ness. His head hit the table, the room fading around him, as unconsciousness stole in mercifully.

FOUR

The sun stung Banner's eyes as he stepped from the boarding-house onto the boardwalk. The morning air felt slightly damp and warm and the sun sparkled from water troughs and glinted off dusty windows. He pressed his lids shut then reopened them, letting his eyes adjust to the brightness. The after-effects of whiskey made his mouth cottony and his tongue spongy. A dull pounding had commenced in his skull. His legs felt shaky, though some of that dissolved as he walked along the boardwalk.

Most townsfolk brushed past him without exchanging a glance, gazes focused straight ahead, though a few shot him cold accusing looks. The new day had not improved the friendliness of Bellstar any, but he reckoned another body showing up riddled with lead hadn't done a lick to enrich their outlook. He couldn't blame them, but they had never been the welcoming sort to begin with. He reckoned he might not have been either had an outlaw gang stormed through his town, and by comparison it wasn't all that different from what two hardcases had done to his life. The town and his future – each had been destroyed by a callous unchangeable force, one that struck quickly and completely, without mercy, and left a body to deal only with the consequences and emptiness that lay in its wake. Bellstar was merely a reflection of what he was, a cold closed thing protecting itself from further devastation.

But Banner was different in a way. Bellstar chose to do nothing, simply carry on about its day to day existence and leave itself open for attack by ignoring the very things that had ravaged it.

Banner didn't ignore what turned him into the thing he was. He went after it, chased it down. Slaughtered it.

Killer. . . .

He stopped, the thought freezing him. He took a deep breath, fighting to keep the pounding in his skull from overwhelming him, then started onward again. Maybe his way wasn't any better, maybe it led to doom as well. The only difference was Bellstar was simply waiting around for the end to come; he was courting it.

Forcing the thought away, he entered the eatery and seated himself at a table near the back. Early risers crowded the place, their talk subdued, almost hushed. Plates clattered and cups clanked against saucers. The cloying aroma of grease and beefsteak and strong coffee ripened the air. He caught the scent of sourdough biscuits and old beans, too, and felt his belly twist with nausea, but only for a moment. He ordered a pot of Arbuckle's, hoping to chase that and the headache away.

Staring out the window, he contemplated his next move. He still had no idea why he had been called to Bellstar, or who had summoned him, and despite the two attempts on his life he wondered if he should just give up and head back to the agency. Likely he had plenty of jobs waiting on him, though he had to admit he had no desire to get at them. He'd give it another couple of days and if no one contacted him he'd figure out what to do then.

He took a gulp of bitter coffee, feeling his head and stomach settle a bit, and thankful for it.

'May I join you, Mr Banner?'

The voice came from behind him and he looked up to see Cynthia Addleson peering at him, her sapphire eyes sparkling in the early morning light coming through the windows. 'Be honored, ma'am.' He half stood, inviting her to sit, and she took a chair. She was wearing a blue day dress with a matching coat that hugged her ample bosom and emphasized the flare of her shapely hips. A small lawn collar encircled her throat and her sleeves hugged her wrists. The trained skirt was trimmed with ruffles and bows. A small locket dangled between her breasts. Fashioned of silver, it was oval, with intricate scroll work. Her hair was worn with a fringe and a Rubens hat. She was stunning, even to his bloodshot eyes, and seeing her again rose something damn near pleasant inside him, some buried need and hope from the past.

She's not Jamie. . . .

His gaze met hers and old feelings stirred again. A whiff of some sort of flowery perfume touched his nostrils and for the briefest of moments his mind jumped back to Jamie, a walk near a creek, her scent filling his senses, her small hand clutching his, and talk of a life together, a ranch of their own. . . .

'Mr Banner?'

He wandered from his thoughts to see her smiling at him and felt an unfamiliar warmth shiver through him. No, that wasn't totally right, was it? Something was familiar about that warmth, but it had been so long ago. . . .

'Ma'am?' was all he could say, feeling suddenly awkward.

'You seem so far away, Mr. Banner. I do hope it's not my company.' Her smile widened, warm as summer sunshine.

He let out an easy laugh, surprised at how freely the expression came. 'Reckon it would never be that, ma'am.'

'Well, good, Mr Banner. I'd be downright crushed if it were.'

The waiter came over and Banner waited while Cynthia declined breakfast and ordered tea.

'Marshal stopped by, Mr Banner.' She paused, taking a sip from her cup. 'Said that man who attacked me was killed.'

Banner nodded. 'He asked me about it, too. Reckon you won't have to worry about him troublin' you again, ma'am. He got what was comin' to him.'

'I'm sure he did, Mr Banner. But I somehow don't think I had much to worry about anyway after you chased them off that way. I never did truly thank you.' She suddenly leaned over and kissed his cheek and the scent of perfume overwhelmed his senses. For a moment he felt lost in it, mind drifting, meandering the trails of the past.

'Luke Banner?' A voice plucked him from his reverie and he looked up, more shaken than he had been in a spell.

A man stood next to their table and Cynthia's face reddened a little with embarrassment. Banner felt his own face heat.

'Help you, gent?' he managed to get out, but it came none to steady.

The man was pompous-looking and jowled, grey peppering his mutton-chop sideburns and bushy mustache. He looked about fifty and Banner judged him to be no threat. His suit looked expensive and a gold chain dangled from a watch pocket. He doffed his Homburg, twisted at its brim.

'May I?' He indicated a nearby chair. Banner nodded and the man dragged the chair close, lowering his bulk into it. He proffered a hand and Banner took it, noting it was damp. The man had something on his mind and the worried set of his eyes told of some problem he wrestled with.

'Name's Wainright Zellers, Mr Banner.' He nodded at Cynthia, as if just noticing she were there. 'Ma'am.'

Cynthia smiled and tilted her head. 'A pleasure, Mr Zellers.'

'Zellers?' Banner ran a hand over his chin. 'Of Zellers' Stage Lines?'

The man gave a nod, chins jiggling. 'That's right, Mr Banner. Finest lines in the West, if I say so myself. None to compare, yessir, none to compare.'

Banner found the man's manner suddenly annoying, though it might have been more for having his breakfast with Cynthia interrupted and the drums in his temples. 'You don't have to sell me, Mr Zellers. Just state your business.'

'Why, no, no, I don't, indeed, Mr Banner. Don't indeed.' The man twisted at his hatband, surprisingly antsy for a big man in more than size. Zellers owned the largest stage line in the territory and had ruthlessly crushed all competition. He had the stench of green and bureaucracy about him and Banner didn't cotton to it a lick. He would have figured a man such as Zellers to never have a frightened thought, but the manhunter felt sure the fellow was saddled with one right now.

The stage line owner's face darkened. He fished in a

pocket, bringing out a small card and flipping it onto the table.

Banner's gaze locked on it and a surprised look filtered into his eyes. It was the size of a business card, but on the front was a red spider stamped in wax. He picked it up, turning it over, seeing red ink on the back that read: Compliments of the Red Widow.

Zellers nodded like a stage with a bad spring. 'The Red Widow Gang, Mr Banner, yessir. They have hit six of my stages so far and I have another one coming from the north in two days. It has, shall we say, a precious cargo that simply must arrive safely. I can't risk this gang attacking it.'

'Gold?' Banner eyed the man, who nodded.

'Gold, Mr Banner, yessir, it is. And too much of it to take a chance with, if you get my meaning.'

Banner nodded, setting the card back down. Cynthia took it, gazing at it a moment, then returned it to the table.

'Too many hits on your stages and folks will pull their business. Your company can't afford that, not with other lines who haven't been robbed waiting to snap up the fares. That the bottom line?'

'Exactly, Mr Banner, exactly. And some of that gold belongs to Zellers' Stage Lines. It is being transferred to a bank in Casper. You can see my predicament.'

Banner cocked an eyebrow. 'You sure the gang will hit it?'

Zellers gave a lusty nod. 'Sure as I am I can't afford them to be successful. They have hit all others lately. This one will be far too rich for them to pass up.'

'All right, Mr Zellers. I see your predicament. But what are you telling me this for? I assume you didn't ride to Bellstar just to bend my ear.'

'No, Mr Banner, I did not. I came to hire you, in fact.

Ask for your help in stopping this gang and saving my company and its reputation. We never suffered a single loss till this gang started up. There's a lot of speculation Zellers' Stage Lines will go belly up with the next robbery and I know for a fact Curtis Cree is waiting to step in and pluck the fruit from the dead vine.'

Banner pondered the man's statement, wondering if this weren't the job he'd been summoned for, though something told him it was not. 'You send me a telegram askin' me to come to Bellstar?'

Zellers looked perplexed. 'Why, no, Mr Banner, I assure you I did not. Just count myself lucky you were close by, yessir, close by.'

'How'd you know I was here?'

Wainright Zellers smiled, but the expression was strained. 'I have a nephew in Bellstar. Told me the great Luke Banner had ridden in, so I seized the opportunity.'

Great was not a word Banner would have used, in fact he rather felt irked by it, as he suspected he might by many things the man said if he stayed around him long. He sized Zellers up in a glance; the man was someone used to getting what he wanted, a man who likely ran his business with an iron hand and controlled each and every minute movement of everyone involved. A man whose heart beat for greenbacks and gold, and little beyond that. Banner supposed he couldn't fault him for such; the West needed men like Zellers to fashion business and provide services, but Banner, though a rich man himself by any standard, never worshipped his bank accounts or set his clock by gold standard time. And now Zellers' world was faced with coming unhinged, his empire crumbling, leaving him a king without a kingdom, and the man was plumb boogered, more so than he was letting on.

Still, Banner had a hard time feeling sorry for him because it was likely the fellow used men like he used his stages, simply employed them to do a job and cared nothing beyond that, discarding them the moment they were no longer useful. Banner had run across too many of his kind, had been hired by the likes and maybe that made him no better than a parasite himself in a way, though he reckoned the thing of vengeance driving him was the true owner of his soul.

Still, Banner might have considered taking the case to preserve the jobs of the men employed by Zellers' Stage Lines, but this man had not sent the telegram and first things came first. There was also the matter of the woman sitting next to him and a sudden desire to be near her. That intrigued him far more than he wanted to admit.

Banner pushed the card back at the businessman, who plucked it from the table and stuffed it in a pocket. 'Reckon I ain't interested at this time, Mr Zellers. I'm sort of waitin' on another case. Sorry I can't help you.'

Zellers' eyes narrowed and Banner saw something close to fury behind them, but it was mixed with vague panic and desperation. He was not a man used to hearing no and it sat as well as sonofabitch stew on a hot day.

'I assure you, Mr Banner, I can reward you handsomely for your efforts, yessir, handsomely. I will double your usual fee, in gold, if need be.'

'I don't need the money, Mr Zellers. I'm not a man who can be bought.' He paused, running a finger over his lip. 'This gang . . . sounds more like you need the Pinkertons or some such. More than one man would be necessary in my estimation.'

Zellers shook his head, the fury remaining behind his eyes, though he controlled it. He needed Banner and would not throw his cards away. 'No, not at all, Mr Banner. One man is needed. One special man I can put on a stage to work from the inside, surprise the gang and bring them down before they know what hit them.'

It sounded vaguely like suicide to Banner and that almost made it more attractive. 'Seems like you could hire regular guards for that.'

'Always do, Mr Banner, but it doesn't seem to make a difference. Gang is prepared for regular guards. Killed a number of them, in fact. I need someone with a bit more savvy than the regular breed. Someone fast and accurate and not afraid to kill.'

Banner felt more irked. 'I ain't your man, Mr Zellers.'
Aren't you?

Zellers peered at Banner and resignation filtered into his eyes. He reached into a pocket, pulling out another card and handing it to Banner, who accepted it. 'I'm staying at my nephew's place, north edge of town. The number is on the back. If you change your mind I will triple your fee.'

'I'm sure Mr Banner's got better things to do with his time than getting himself killed for your company, Mr Zellers,' Cynthia said, speaking for the first time. Her blue eyes went from Banner to the stage line owner, a look of concern on her face.

Zellers grunted, heaving himself out of the chair. 'Getting killed isn't what I had in mind, ma'am. Killing is. Good day.' The heavy-set man nodded to her and then to Banner, placing his Homburg atop his head. He ambled towards the door and Banner watched him go, wondering if he hadn't been too hasty in turning Zellers down and if the man's offer wasn't the diversion he needed.

'You're thinking of taking that job, Mr Banner, aren't you?'

He looked over at Cynthia, seeing the concern on her face had deepened. He shrugged. 'Maybe I said no too quickly.'

She peered at him intently, searching behind his eyes and he felt everything inside him want to open, reveal itself. It was a feeling he wasn't used to, had not felt in a very long time and it frightened him. 'What are you, Mr Banner?' she asked, voice lowering. '*Who* are you?'

He almost laughed though he saw goddamn little humor in the question. 'Who is maybe not so important, ma'am. What . . . well, that's another story. I hire out to kill folks. It ain't pretty, but that is the only way I can put it.'

'A manhunter, Mr Banner?'

He looked at her, hearing no condemnation in her voice and that was something new for him. Most folks who knew what he did, even those who hired him, treated him with a sort of nervous respect, a look that said though they needed his services they condemned what he did and the man behind it, branding him something different from other men. It was the respect a man gave a rattler, knowing nature somehow needed the ugly beast but also frightened it would strike or kill at a moment's inclination.

Cynthia didn't look at him that way. He saw something else in her eyes, but what it was he couldn't put a finger to. It might have been understanding, or acceptance. Whatever it was, he knew only that it was different in a way that didn't displease him.

'Most folks would call me a killer, ma'am. Some say I got no soul.'

She smiled. 'I wouldn't say that, Mr Banner. Not at all. I can see something in your eyes, something hurt and struggling, some need you can't come to terms with.'

Her words startled him and he felt suddenly more uncomfortable than he ever had. She had read him perfectly, too perfectly, and he wondered if he had simply lost the ability to hide it, the way he was losing his reflexes.

'I've offended you, Mr Banner.' A warm smile turned her lips. 'I didn't mean to. I'm sorry.'

He shook his head. 'No, ma'am, I don't think you could offend me if you tried. Perhaps I just ain't used to folks being so forthright.'

Her eyes took his and for a moment he wanted to fall into them, saw Jamie's face over hers and saw the skeletons of what he could have been.

Her hand slid over his and the look in her eyes turned to compassion, whatever it was before lost in the depths of sapphire. 'And you're wrong, Mr Banner. Who you are *is* important, important to me. I want to know you, Mr Banner. I want to know who and what you are and what makes you do what you do.'

Banner felt a sinking in his belly, yet at the same time he had no desire to pull his hand from beneath hers.

Jamie. . . .

'You don't want to know me that way, ma'am. It's a downright ugly sight.'

Her smile lost some of its guilelessness and she squeezed his hand. 'Oh, but I do, Mr Banner. It seems like I have wanted to know you for a very long time.'

'You just met me yesterday, ma'am.'

'Oh, but I met you so long ago in my dreams, Mr Banner. And dreams don't die so easy.'

Banner pulled his hand back and straightened. This woman before him did things to him no woman since Jamie had, made him almost want to hope for something better, something new, something so far removed from what he had become. It frightened him, more than any job he had ever signed onto, and, he had a feeling, more than any he ever would. He wondered more powerfully if he shouldn't have snapped up Zellers' offer, used it as an excuse to avoid the things screaming inside his soul. One thing he felt sure of: he knew now he could not really have pulled the trigger last night in his room. Because from the moment he had met Cynthia Addleson he had found a reason to go on besides vengeance.

FIVE

'Have you ever been in love, Mr Banner?' Cynthia Addleson turned her head towards him as they walked along the boardwalk towards the hotel.

The question jolted him and for an instant Jamie's face flashed in his mind. His eyes took on a distant look and he felt strangely lost, the sadness that was always inside him welling, burning, haunting.

He drew a deep breath and stared straight ahead at the boardwalk, pausing long moments before answering. 'Reckon I have, once. It was . . . a long time ago.'

'I knew you had, Mr Banner. I could tell. You got that look of someone who knew love . . . and maybe lost it.'

He glanced at her and saw something in her sapphire eyes, and again he couldn't tell what it was, but it was there, plain as day. The look vanished as quickly and she smiled and he wondered how she had become so perceptive. She seemed to know him as well as he knew himself. They had talked for over an hour in the café after Zellers left and he had found her charming, beguiling. He had also felt his defences lowering. She reminded him of Jamie so much it seemed natural to answer her questions, laugh with her, relax. Jamie had always brought that out of him, and Cynthia had that way, too. Jamie seemed to know every corner of his soul and that might have been the thing he loved about her the most.

How would Jamie feel, now? How would she feel if she knew what you did, how you butchered every hard-case you came across because you can't live with not saving her that day? You felt helpless then and you still do. You always will because you're too goddamn bull-headed to see you're slipping and the thing inside of you is dying, making it harder to go on, harder to hold the devil in a bottle. It wants to take you with it. It damn near did last night.

He gave a slight shiver despite the warmth of the day, and when he came from his thoughts he saw the young woman gazing at him, as if searching for something behind his eyes.

'What is it, Mr Banner? What's wrong?'

He shook his head. 'Nothing's wrong, ma'am. Just was . . . recollectin', I reckon.'

Her face turned serious and the indefinable something drifted back into her eyes, as quickly vanishing. 'You loved her deeply, didn't you?'

He nodded, an ache commencing in his heart. 'Yes, I did. More than anything. We were . . . to be married.'

Cynthia Addleson paused and the sound of their steps clomping on the boards rang hollowly in his ears. 'She died, didn't she?'

The words stung, though by God he knew he should be used to it. It had been years since that day but goddamn if it didn't feel like it had been just last week. He nodded, voice lowering. 'Yes, she . . . was killed.'

Cynthia's face turned serious, understanding. 'I'm sorry, Mr Banner. It's a terrible thing, death, I mean.' She stopped and touched his arm and he halted, looking at her, seeing sympathy and compassion on her features. 'I lost someone, too, Mr Banner.'

His eyes locked with hers and he saw pain, the same pain he felt, the pain she allowed him to see, and he got the impression she didn't allow that to many. Her fingers played at her locket and a tear slid from her eye. 'You been married, ma'am?' was all he could think of asking. He had never faced his own loss, what could he possibly say to comfort hers?

'No . . . no, I ain't never been. Reckon I'm gettin' past the age for it, but it don't rightly matter. See my ma and pa died when I was little, killed in an Indian raid. I never really knew them. My brother was ten years older than me and he raised me and my sister like we were his own children. He got a job as a 'hand for some rich man who owned a big cattle spread, made enough to get us by and give us a few things like dolls and even a bottle of perfume once. I 'spect he might have got it from consorting with certain women, but it didn't rightly matter. I was happy with it, as happy as could be.' She paused and Banner ducked his chin at the boardwalk. She slid her arm through his and they started forward. A confusion of feelings washed over him. He couldn't deny how good it felt to be touched by a woman, especially Cynthia Addleson, yet at the same time he felt guilt and fear take him. He had been with certain women, though not for a spell, but somehow they had never posed a threat to Jamie's memory, being the type they were. They filled lonely nights, kept the nightmares away if only for a few hours. He had never felt as if he were betraying her. But with Cynthia it was different. She got inside him, stirred things he'd thought dead, and he wondered if Jamie could ever forgive him.

'What happened to him, ma'am?'

'Wish you'd stop callin' me ma'am, Mr Banner. Please call me by my proper name.' She smiled warmly at him.

He couldn't help smiling back. 'Only if you call me
Luke instead of Mr Banner.'

She giggled. 'It's a deal – Luke. I much prefer that
anyhow.' After a pause, her face turned grim again and
her voice came lower. 'He was killed, Luke. Murdered.
For no good reason. Man who did it left his body by a
creek for the buzzards.' A note of bitter anger laced her
voice and he reckoned he didn't blame her a bit. Jamie
had been killed beside a creek, too, and even if the
similarity ended there the pain and dread loss were
the same.

'I'm sorry. . . .' It came out almost a whisper. He
couldn't say any more, because words simply didn't
matter. They didn't help, provided no comfort, could
never remove the empty feeling death left in its wake.

She tried a smile. 'Well, it was a long time ago. Reckon
I've learned to live with it. But my brother, he raised me
right and I have him to thank for that. Wouldn't be the
woman I am today if'n it weren't for him.'

As they reached the hotel entrance, Luke Banner
paused and looked at Cynthia Addleson. Despite the
pain on her face and sorrow staining her eyes, she
looked absolutely a vision in the morning sunlight. Her
hair glowed like polished gold and the soft curve of her
slightly parted lips was inviting. But he saw something
else again, though he still could not put a peg to it. One
thing he did light on: something he noticed in her
speech. She spoke precisely most of the time but occasionally lapsed into a more local vernacular and he
reckoned she was a lovely combination of woman and
the girl raised by a lone brother. She was a wonder in
his estimation and a sudden startling notion entered
his mind:

I could fall in love with you. . . .

No, that was impossible. He could never love

anyone. It was too dangerous and he'd be damned if he'd suffer another loss.

His gaze focused back on her and she smiled. 'A penny for your thoughts, Mr . . . *Luke*.'

He grinned, embarrassed, as if she had somehow seen what was in his mind reflected in his eyes. 'Reckon just it's my turn to ask you: What kind of a woman are you, Cynthia Addleson? *Who* are you?'

'Why, what do you mean?' Her eyes widened slightly and her lips looked ripe and beckoning. He suppressed an urge to take her in his arms and kiss her.

'Just that you seem . . . different from other women I've known. You're educated, I can tell by the way you speak and act, probably highly so. That ain't always the opportunity for a woman in these parts. Yet sometimes you lapse back into a familiar speech pattern. You're courageous, too. Most folks wouldn't be inclined to go walkin' about after an attack like the one that occurred yesterday. You have a perceptiveness and style about you that's. . . .'

What, Banner? Wholly enticing? More intoxicating than that polluted rotgut you drown your memories in?

She touched his arm and he felt a shiver wander through him. 'What, Luke? Please tell me.'

He shrugged. 'Reckon there's just something different about you. Can't rightly put my finger to it.'

She smiled. 'I hope it is something you like, I truly do.'

He nodded, unable to hide the fact. 'I shorely do, Miss Cynthia. You're a right fine lady, if I'm not being too forward.'

She laughed as they reached the hotel and stepped into the lobby. The interior was furnished in sparse fashion, a few hardbacked chairs and a medallion-backed sofa that had seen better days. The chandelier could have used some cleaning if the thick coating of dust and cobwebs were any indication. The carpet was threadbare and stained. Bellstar's hostelry was hardly the epitome of style and class, but since it was the town's only it could be what it wanted and Banner reckoned it was as comfortable as any, though maybe not befitting a woman as classy as Cynthia Addleson.

They walked to the stairs, the hotel man behind the desk keeping his head buried in a pulp novel, and began going up.

'I went to school in the East for a spell, Luke. My brother had saved enough money to give us a comfortable means. My sister fell in love with a man from Arizona way and married him, leaving me on my own. I had little choice but to school myself, though even five years East didn't quite take the West out of me. I learned design and came back to Wyoming, started a little dress shop and it did right well for the last few years. Then I got lonesome. I guess there were just too many memories there for me, so I decided I'd move closer to my sister and start another shop there. Reckon there ain't much more to me than that, Luke.'

They paused upon reaching the door to her room and she turned to him, eyes soft and pleading and suddenly he wanted to hold her, feel her close to him.

'Reckon that's enough by a damn sight, Miss Cynthia.'

She smiled. 'Good, I'm glad. Because I can't rightly live with the ghosts any more, Luke. I don't like being alone with them.'

He nodded, a distant look crossing his eyes. He knew all too well what she meant and he reckoned he could no longer live with his. She leaned forward and her lips brushed his. He felt waves of heat rush through his body. When she stepped back she turned to her door, unlocking it and letting it swing inward, then turned back to him.

'I'd like to see you again, Luke. I have a week in Bellstar and I'd like to spend it with you, if'n you're agreeable. . . .'

He wanted to say there was nothing he would like better, but the darkness inside him rose up, telling him he could not risk this woman's life. Two attempts had been made on him and he felt positive there would be others.

He sighed. 'Reckon it might not be to your advantage to be seen with me, Miss Cynthia. I don't get close to folks, not since I became what I am—'

'Shhh.' She placed her finger to his lips, silencing him. 'You're a man, Luke. Nothing more. A man I find attractive and interesting and want to spend what time I have here with. I had to fend for myself for so long, and my brother raised me as tough as he was himself, despite what you see. I don't run in fear from possibilities, just like I won't let that attack yesterday keep me from living my life.'

Banner held her gaze, saw the seriousness in her eyes. She was telling the truth; this woman was afraid of nothing and he damn well admired that.

He turned, started to walk away, then looked back at her. 'You're a hell of a woman, Cynthia Addleson.'

And you remind me so very much of another. . . .

She smiled warmly. 'I'll be at the café for dinner at five sharp, Luke. I don't expect to be dining alone.' She stepped into her room and closed the door and he knew despite his protests he would be there.

You're a damn fool, Banner. You're risking her life and you know it.

Luke Banner leaned on the rail outside the hotel

and cursed himself for letting Cynthia Addleson fill his thoughts. He wondered if he could have stopped it if he tried and reckoned it had now become impossible. He would meet her for dinner, but that had to be it. He couldn't expose her to his life, such as it was. Every moment more she spent with him meant the possibility of death for her. Already two hardcases had attempted to bury him. It would happen again, he felt sure of it, as he felt sure he was falling in love with her.

You're a fool, Banner. A goddamn fool! You'll be her death the way you were Jamie's. . . .

Jamie's face rose in his mind and he shook his head, the guilt of not being able to save her that day turning in his belly.

What of Cynthia Addleson? If he did expose her to the threat that stalked him everywhere could he save her? Could he prevent what he couldn't with Jamie?

No, he could barely keep himself alive, though he was forced to admit he struggled with a subconscious wish to die.

You can go somewhere. Banner, change your name, way you thought.

Again the thought danced in his mind but again he shot it down. As long as he was alive someone would find him, sometime, somewhere and that would be that. He would not be expecting it and the end would come suddenly and violently as it did to most gunfighters. A bullet in the back of the head or a strike from the dark. It would happen and he knew it.

If he were alive. . . .

A fleeting notion took him but he quickly forced it away. What was he thinking? Was a life on some farm really for him? It had been once, a very long time ago, but was it now?

Maybe. With a woman like Cynthia Addleson.

He pushed himself away from the rail, a heavy sigh escaping his lips. The thoughts spun in his mind and for one of the few times he could recollect he felt confused and directionless. Struggling against what he wanted and what he knew. Against every ghost of every man he had killed, against the bloodstained memory of Jamie dead in his arms. Before, his only direction had been vengeance, retribution. What was it now?

He stepped from the boardwalk, crossing the street as a buckboard rattled past, wheels throwing up clouds of dust that settled over rails and left films in water troughs. His mind went to the café and to Zellers and what the man had told him about the Red Widow Gang. The prospect of being busy on a case was suddenly more attractive to him than it had been just hours ago and maybe that was the coward's way out. But it was familiar, a trail travelled and one that delayed making any decisions he would have to live – and die – with.

He had to admit he was getting downright antsy waiting on whoever had called him here, waiting for the next attempt on his life. As he stepped onto the opposite boardwalk, he stopped and took out the card Zellers had given him, peering at the name of Zellers' Stage Lines, then tucking it back into his pocket. Maybe that *was* the diversion he needed. It would buy him time, give him a focus and maybe it was slightly less dangerous than sitting in his room with a bottle of rotgut and a Peacemaker handy.

On impulse, he walked to the marshal's office and stepped inside. Marshal Hart looked up from behind his desk and Banner nodded.

The marshal's brow scrunched. 'Surprised to see you here, Banner. Hope you ain't come to tell me there's another body lyin' somewhere.'

Banner shook his head. 'Hope it don't come to that.'
He lowered himself onto the hardbacked chair.

The marshal chuckled. 'Don't go bettin' your grub-
stake on it.'

'Never do, Marshal.'

'Oh, no?' The marshal cocked an eyebrow, but
Banner ignored the remark.

He plucked the card from his pocket and tossed it on
the desk. The marshal looked at it and nodded. 'Reckon
you're familiar with the name,' Luke said.

'Ain't everyone? Man's a pompous mule but he ain't
got a lick of competition in these parts – least he didn't
till his stages started getting hit regularly. Now folks
are gettin' a mite fidgety and startin' to look elsewhere.
Reckon one more hit and our Mr Zellers will be
thinkin' on a new line of work.'

Banner nodded. 'That's pretty much the way he sees
it. He tried to hire me.'

The marshal grinned. 'Don't say? Well, there's your
callin', Banner.'

Luke shook his head. 'No, he claimed he wasn't the
one to send the telegram. Said he heard from his
nephew I was in town.'

The marshal harrumphed. 'Then you ain't any closer
to knowin' than you were.'

'Maybe not, but after a spell in my line of work you
learn sometimes things you think don't connect do.'

'You thinkin' of takin' him up on it, then?'

Banner gave a noncommittal shrug. 'What do you
know about this Red Widow Gang?'

'Not a hell of a lot more than I told you. They've hit
all around the area, robbing stages, banks, jewelry
stores, what have you, but never Bellstar. Like I said,
folks keep damn little around to make that prospect
attractive.'

'Anyone ever seen them and live to tell about it?'

'Heard tell one guard said a few words before he went boots up. Gang dresses all in black, with black hoods, 'cept for a red poncho-type thing worn over their shoulders. They hit hard and fast, and ain't partial to survivors. They leave little cards with the wax seal of a spider, reckon just to mock the law. That's all I know.'

Banner nodded, standing. 'Zellers said he has a stage comin' in soon with a big gold shipment.'

'Reckon that's mighty attractive to the likes of the Red Widow Gang if they get wind of it.'

Banner plucked the card from the desk and stuck it in his pocket. 'Reckon it is.'

'You goin' to see Zellers?'

Banner nodded. 'I got a mind to.' He walked towards the door, clasping the handle and opening it.

'Cynthia Addleson's a beautiful woman, Banner. . . .' he heard the marshal say behind him.

Banner turned, eyeing the man. 'What are you gettin' at, Marshal?'

The marshal chuckled. 'Word gets around, even in a town like Bellstar, Banner. You could do worse and she's likely a hell of a lot less dangerous than chasin' a gang like the Red Widow.'

Banner grinned. 'Depends on your perspective . . .'

A knock banged on the door and Henkins jolted. He lay on a bunk in the corner of the saloon's back room, where his mysterious employer had told him to hide out and await word on when he would ride with the gang on the next job. The waiting had been driving him plumb loco, but upon hearing the knock he reckoned there were worse things.

He slowly swung his feet from the bunk and stared at the door, as if whoever stood behind it were the

Devil. He reckoned that wasn't a damn sight far from the truth.

'Who is it?' he asked and no one answered. He eased himself off the bunk and went to the door, grasping the handle. Sweat streaked down his face and his heart stuttered.

He pulled the door inward and peered out, but the small hallway was empty and he felt puzzled for a moment, about to close the door when he noticed a piece of folded paper at his feet. He knelt, retrieving it, then closed the door softly. Opening the paper, he saw words scrawled across it in red ink, instructions he was to follow, and his belly sank. Within the folded paper was also a card, a thing stamped with red wax and the seal of a spider. . . .

Luke Banner stepped out into the day and began to walk along the boardwalk, gaze alert and searching for any prospect of a threat. He spotted none and his trail-honed sixth sense remained silent. He hoped that hadn't suddenly decided to desert him.

Relaxing, he pondered the brief conversation he'd had with the marshal. The lawdog was right about Cynthia, perhaps too right, because what he suggested was likely the very reason Banner found himself considering taking Zellers' job. She was dangerous to him, and to herself, if she got near him too often. Not the same type of danger the Red Widow Gang posed, but maybe something entirely worse. A danger to all he had become, to the demon of vengeance inside him.

You're running again, Banner. Way you always have, from Jamie's memory and from a woman who might offer you a chance at something besides the hell you exist in.

Maybe he was. But damned if he could stop himself.

Approaching the house near the edge of town that was indicated on the back of the business card, he paused. It was a two-storey affair, ritzy as far as dwellings in Bellstar went, and likely that was because Zellers provided his nephew with the means to make it so. The front was neatly kept, with a flower bed that showed a woman's touch and ruffled blue curtains in the parlor window framed by neat white shutters. The whole thing gave off an atmosphere of tranquillity, but something felt suddenly wrong. A tingle of apprehension shivered through his nerves. A few steps closer and the feeling grew stronger. That sixth sense had not deserted him; it came sharp as a whore's tongue now. Nothing looked overtly out of place, in fact quite the opposite. Yet he couldn't deny the premonition of danger, nor could he ignore it. It had saved his life too many times.

He eased towards the porch, angling to the right, alert for the slightest movement or sign of trouble. His heart picked up a beat, his blood raced through his veins. His hand twitched and he felt the darkness inside him wanting to take over, guide him.

Death is waiting behind that door, Banner, maybe your own. . . .

Reaching the porch he stepped onto it with as little noise as possible and pressed himself against the wall, listening. He heard nothing, no motion from inside, no signs of life and that made something sink in his belly.

You're too late.

He grasped the door handle, turning it ever so slowly, then letting the door creak inward. He waited, wondering if a shot would come, counting to twenty before chancing a look inside.

He saw nothing in the entryway, heard no sound, and eased around the corner into the house. Pausing, he listened again then went forward.

Death's been here, Banner. You can feel it. You'd know that ugly bastard anywhere, the chill He leaves. . . .

He suppressed the urge to shudder and moved deeper into the house, gaze searching every corner and cranny for any threat. At first he saw nothing, no sign of life. The entryway was decorated with very little, a medallion chair and settee, a chandelier with considerably less dust than the one at the hotel. A few pictures of stagecoaches adorned the striped paper walls. Nothing looked disturbed or out of place. He shook his head, the feeling of apprehension strengthening despite the lack of obvious threat.

A moment later he discovered his initial trepidation was dead right.

Entering the parlor, he froze. A body lay on the floor, arm outstretched, grasping at nothing. Blonde hair spread out beneath a woman's head, stained with crimson. A scarlet puddle was slowly spreading across the hardwood floor. Her blue eyes stared sightlessly upward.

'Jamie. . . .' he whispered, waves of grief rushing through him as he saw her there, lying dead all over again.

No, not her. It's not her. It can't be. Look again.

His vision focused and he realized the woman's blonde hair was of a darker shade, her figure more robust than Jamie's. Only one thing matched: she was equally as dead. A bullet had blasted a chunk off her forehead and splattered pieces of her skull and spongy brain matter across the floor.

Sickened, Banner's gaze jumped around the room, seeing no sign of the killer. His hand went to his Peacemaker, sliding it noiselessly from its holster. He guessed the woman was likely Zellers' niece by marriage. The corpse looked fresh.

Was the murderer still in the house?

Alarm rang louder in Banner's mind and every fiber told him the danger was close by, still in the house. He backed from the parlor, looking towards the stairs that led to a second-floor landing. He moved towards them, heart starting to pound, hand loose and ready with the Peacemaker.

It's up there Banner: Death. It's waiting for you. . . .

He took the stairs slowly, placing each foot carefully to avoid a creak, though a couple came anyway. The heaviness of death crushed him, now, and he could feel apprehension cinching his belly as he reached the landing.

A series of doors lined the hall and one near the end stood open, as if inviting him in. He moved towards it, gaze sweeping back and forth, senses tingling with danger.

A sound reached his ears and he stopped dead. It came from the open room, the sound of boots scuffing across the floor. Someone was still here as he suspected and Banner would have laid odds it wasn't Zellers or his nephew. If either were here he doubted they'd be in much better shape than the woman in the parlor.

He went forward, redoubling his efforts at stealth. Reaching the door, he eased just inside and levered his gun. A man crouched over another body, the body of Wainright Zellers. The stage-line owner had a gaping hole in his chest and blood had splashed across the hardwood in gruesome patterns. The air carried the stench of a slaughterhouse, coppery blood and sour internals. The man hunched over the body was rifling through pockets.

'Stand up and turn towards me, slowlike,' Banner levered his gun on the man's back.

He saw the killer jolt, then slowly rise and turn.

Banner recognized him instantly as the other man from the alley, the one holding Cynthia. 'You—'

Something lunged at him from the side and he tried to jerk back, but was not entirely successful. A lamp bounced from his temple and sent his senses reeling. The Peacemaker flew from his hand and he slammed into the door frame, stumbled back. He realized too late the killer had another partner, one who must have heard some slight sound Banner had made and placed himself out of sight behind the doorway. Banner would have cursed his foolish error in judgement but was too busy trying to keep his feet.

The hardcase immediately pounced, trying to club Banner's brains out with a blocky fist. The manhunter barely managed to avoid the full impact of the blow and that mostly because he was stumbling backward and the man had mistimed it.

Banner lost his precarious balance and his feet went out from under him. He went down, landing on his rear. The hardcase charged him, obviously intending to prevent the manhunter from gaining his feet and resetting.

Banner struggled to focus, caught sight of a huge blur descending on him and instinctively jerked his feet up. His boots slammed into the man's belly and the hardcase let out an explosive burst of air. Banner thrust his legs and the hardcase flew backwards.

The manhunter twisted, pressing his palms against the floor, and struggled to push himself up. As he gained hands and knees, a boot buried itself in his ribs and he felt a spiderweb of pain career through his chest and side. He crumpled, gasping, finding it hard to get air. His senses wanted to desert him, fade into merciful blackness.

No, he refused to let himself pass out. If he did he

would be at the mercy of the hardcases and that would mean certain death. He had to gain his feet, fight back. . . .

A swish of clothing caught his attention, told him the man was delivering another kick. He rolled sideways instinctively in an attempt to avoid a blow that might finish him.

The man who'd been crouched over the body had delivered the kick. His boot glanced from Banner's arm, as the manhunter went sideways, but did little damage.

Banner stopped his roll and looked up to see the hardcase rushing towards him again. The first attacker had recovered and was coming forward.

Banner was a strong man, and in his younger days he might have recovered more quickly than he did now, but he still had enough left to do the job. He summoned all that strength and hoisted himself to his feet, albeit not as gracefully as he once might have.

The hardcases looked momentarily surprised he had managed the feat after getting his ribs kicked in, but recovered almost immediately and lunged at him.

The first attacker went for his Smith & Wesson and Banner delivered a spinning side kick that caught the man's hand as it pulled the gun free. The pistol flew out of his grip and spun across the landing floor.

The hardcase from the alley slammed into Banner then, sent the manhunter crashing into the wall. The impact drove the air from his lungs and he had all he could do to keep his senses.

He brought his knee up as the man came in, catching the hardcase south of the border. The fellow let out a bellow and doubled over in pain, clutching his personals. Banner stepped away from the wall and jerked a sharp uppercut that lifted the man off his feet and he pitched backwards, crashing onto the floor on his back, groaning, blood dribbling from his mouth.

The manhunter spent a fraction too long surveying his work, something he would have never done in his younger days.

A mistake.

That instant gave the first man the opportunity to set himself and strike. He careened into Banner with the impact of a bull. Banner was hurled sideways, unable to halt his stumble. Something hit his side and gave with a loud *crack*! and he kept going. With a crash of realization he knew he had struck the landing rail and was going right on through it!

He twisted, but it was too late. He grabbed at the chandelier, catching hold of its edge with his fingertips and for an instant seemed suspended in mid-air.

His fingers jerked free, the momentum too much and the precarious hold too little. He plunged downward, the floor rushing up to meet him a hell of a lot faster than he would have liked.

SIX

Banner slammed into the floor and a curtain of multi-colored lights exploded before his vision. Blackness crept in from the corners of his mind and he had the urge to just let it overwhelm him, lead him to some safe place where pain and death no longer existed.

He'll kill you, Banner. . . .

So?

What did he care? He had almost done the job himself and something inside sure as hell seemed to wish just that.

Cynthia. . . .

Her face rose in his mind, blue eyes shining, laughing, beckoning. Then Jamie's formed. Images of that day at the creek, her death, tracking down the man who had hired her killers, the years of killing and death and vengeance streamed through his mind, ending with the attack on Cynthia in the alley by one of the men who attacked him here.

He might kill her, Banner. You have to get him first. You have to punish him, make him pay for killing Jamie, make them all pay over and over again until you've wiped the stain clean from your bastard soul. . . .

Banner's thoughts struggled to connect. This man

hadn't killed Jamie; he'd attacked Cynthia. No, they had all killed her, every last goddamn one of them; that was why Luke Banner existed, that was the dark force that drove him on, forced him to kill and kill.

And kill.

You can't let him kill Cynthia, too. You can't take that chance. . . .

Banner fought to clear his head, some bastard will to go on dragging him into full awareness. Blurred vague shapes and patches of light wavered before his eyes and distantly he heard a clomping rhythm – the sound of boots descending the stairs to his left. The killer, coming to finish the job.

A burst of desperate determination flowed through the manhunter as his vision focused. He lay staring up at the chandelier, a pounding in his head, pain ringing from every corner of his body. He felt a thin snake of blood trickling from the corner of his mouth.

At first he couldn't move, only hear the sound of the boots getting closer, boots that meant his doom, the end he might have prayed for for too many years. Consciousness threatened to desert him again, but some shred of will made him hold on.

He lifted his head, twisting it left, and saw the man from the alley approaching him as though he were approaching a sleeping bear. The other hardcase, the one who had shoved him through the rail, followed a few steps behind.

The one who had pushed him let out a sharp laugh. 'He ain't so goddamn tough, Henkins. Fact, we got him right easy, I reckon. All reputation, I told yer so.'

Henkins shook his head, a grim look on his face, along with a shadow of fear. 'Hell he is! I saw him in action – twice. You mighta got plumb lucky, but you best not take your lookers off him.'

The other scoffed. 'Hell's bells, he's a polecat without a stink. He ain't goin' nowhere 'cept straight to hell. Leastwise he will after I put lead twixt his winders.'

Henkins shot the man a withering look. 'You go to the alley outside the saloon. There's a back door and our employer will be waitin' on word 'bout Zellers. Tell 'im the old mule's taken care of and won't be tryin' to hire on any more manhunters to track down the Red Widow Gang. Tell 'im Banner's been taken care of, too. I'll join you there in five minutes.'

'Reckon we'll get a bonus for this?' The other looked hopeful, hard face gleaming with greed.

Henkins let out a humorless laugh. 'Hell, yes – we'll get to live.'

The man grumbled but headed towards the rear, disappearing. Henkins eased a step closer to Banner, looking none the more confident the manhunter wouldn't suddenly spring up and punch his ticket.

Banner fought to summon every last ounce of strength, lift himself from the floor. Bolts of pain skewered his ribs and skull. His senses whirled, then jerked still. He managed to get propped up on his elbows, but his body felt leaden, unable to respond the way it should have. He was still too stunned to move and he stared up at the man named Henkins.

The hardcase had his Smith & Wesson aimed at Banner's head. 'Ain't nothin' personal, Banner,' he muttered and Banner heard a measure of fear and respect in the killer's voice. 'But it's me or you and I reckon I ain't never been the selfless sort.'

The hardcase inched the iron forward and Banner, helpless, saw death staring at him from the hollow of a .44. The manhunter knew death would catch up to him some day and now that day had come. As soon as the hardcase squeezed the trigger lead would plough into his skull and he would be with Jamie. The notion was almost inviting.

But something inside refused to die without a fight. If his life were going to end it would not end passively; he reckoned that fact was plain the night he couldn't pull the trigger in his room.

By pure instinct he threw every last bit of strength into a sideways roll towards the hardcase. He hoped to hit the man's legs hard enough to knock him off balance, though he knew that would probably just delay the inevitable.

It was a slim hope, a dying hope. And it failed.

Explosions of pain wracked his body with the move and he didn't quite make it onto his side. He was still too weak.

The hardcase let out a nervous breath and adjusted his aim.

A shot thundered through the room and Banner braced himself for the burning punch of lead and sudden blackness that would follow. He said no prayers, for he doubted God listened to the likes of a man who had killed so many under a guise of perverted justice.

But blackness never came.

Instead the hardcase's face twisted with a shocked look and a second shot rang out as the man reflexively jerked his trigger. Lead ploughed into the floor fractions of an inch beside Banner's face. The bullet buried itself in the hardwood. A sliver flew up and ripped across his cheek, but that was the extent of the damage.

The hardcase pitched backward and went down. He slammed into the floor, lay still. His Smith & Wesson skidded across the boards.

Heart pounding in his throat, Banner forced himself to turn, spikes of pain stabbing his chest and ribs and back. He saw Marshal Hart poised in the doorway, Peacemaker smoking in his hand.

'Any more of 'em?' he asked, peering at Banner.

Banner nodded, the move bringing renewed intensity to the pounding in his head. 'One. Went out the back.'

The marshal nodded and holstered his gun. 'Saw him. Was on my way to the eatery when I noticed him sneakin' around from the back. Knew you were comin' here so I figured I'd better take me a looksee. Lucky for you I did.'

Banner tried a smile that didn't work. 'Zellers' niece is in the parlor, dead. The old man's upstairs.'

The marshal nodded and stepped close to Banner, surveying him. 'We best get you to the doc's. You look like hell.'

'Ain't news to me, Marshal.' Banner paused, getting himself propped on his side and nudging his head at the landing. 'My gun's still up there. . . .'

'I'll have my deputy get it later. Gotta take me a look at Zellers, too, then get the 'taker over here.' The marshal scooched, clamping an arm around Banner's back, and hoisted the manhunter to his feet. Pain screaming through every conceivable point in his body, Banner was amazed he could even stand, though he had a moment where he thought that might not last.

The marshal wrapped a bracing arm around Banner and led him towards the door.

An hour later he lay in a bed in the back of the doc's, the marshal standing nearby, hat in hand. The doc, a middle-aged man with a thick unkempt beard and all the bedside manner of an unpaid bardove had wrapped Banner's ribs and forced him to swallow a dose of laudanum that tasted just slightly better than the marshal's six-gun coffee. He had gotten lucky, in more ways than one. He had his life, thanks to the marshal, and nothing was broken, though he would suffer numerous bruises and a good measure of stiffness for a few days.

'Lucky for you you got a hide tougher than a buffalo and the constitution of one to boot.' The doc shook his head. 'That fall mighta plumb kilt a weaker man.'

Banner wondered if luck had anything to do with it. He had a notion fate might have something worse in mind and this was just another signpost he was getting closer to his destination, the place where Death would be waiting. 'Much obliged for you fixin' me up, doc,' he said, but the truth of it was everything hurt like hellfire, despite the opiate in his system, and he wondered if dyin' might not have been a good deal easier.

The doc sighed, shaking his head. 'Don't know what the hell for. Fella like you'll just get yer fool hide shot clean full of holes sooner or later anyhow. Won't be able to do a damn thing 'bout that.' With that the doc shuffled from the room. Banner turned towards the marshal, a resigned expression on his face.

'Reckon he might be right, Banner.' The marshal hesitated then added, 'You figure they knew you were goin' there?'

Banner shook his head, the move bringing instant pain and he let out a mumbled curse. 'Don't see as how. You were the only one I told. Reckon they just got lucky.'

The marshal's brow scrunched. 'Don't know 'bout that, Banner. You been involved in too many attacks already though admittedly those might be unrelated and just the usual fare for you. Somethin' don't rightly cipher up, though, especially with Zellers askin' you to take on the Red Widow Gang. Someone wanted him dead and I reckon that might be the reason.'

' 'Cause he tried to hire me. . . .' It was more a statement than a question, because Banner had the same notion, though other things still didn't quite make sense.

The marshal nodded. 'That's the way I'm lookin' at it.'

'That don't make the other incidents related, Marshal. I got the feelin' Trombley was settin' me up, but I might be wrong. Rotgut'll hornswoggle a man's thinkin' sometimes.'

The marshal chuckled. 'That might be the case, but I reckon you ain't lived this long by not listenin' to your hunches.'

Banner was forced to agree. The more he chewed it the more he reckoned Trombley had ulterior motives and had lured Banner into that gunfight. But the second attempt he might be dead wrong about. Those men were attacking Cynthia and it was pure coincidence he had come along at that time.

Wasn't it?

Something pricked at his suspicions, it might have been some subtle look on the hardcase's face as he turned towards Banner with the knife, or it might have been a creeping paranoia brought about by too many past attempts on his life. He couldn't be certain and with a shot of laudanum didn't have much mind to dwell on it.

'My hunch tells me there's more to this than we're seein', Marshal. That man you killed was the other who attacked Cynthia in the alley.'

The marshal's face took on a look of surprise. 'Henkins?'

Banner nodded, the movement a little less painful this time. 'You're acquainted with the fella?'

The marshal shrugged. 'Seen him around. Hardcase

to be sure, but kept his nose mostly clean till now. Had me a feelin' he was up to no good but could never catch him at anything.'

The doc came back into the room, carrying Banner's Peacemaker, a look of disdain on his face. 'S'pose you'll be wantin' this, though God knows why almost gettin' killed ain't opened your eyes. Deputy brought it.' He handed it to Banner and Banner carefully maneuvered himself around and slid it into the holster piled on the hardbacked chair next to him. 'Obliged, doc.'

'Don't go thankin' me for nothin' like that.' The doc shook his head, disapproval plain, then peered at the marshal. 'He needs rest. Appreciate it if you'd take your business elsewhere for the time bein'.'

The marshal nodded and set his hat atop his head.

'Marshal, do me a favor?' Banner asked, as the lawman started for the door.

Hart stopped, raising an eyebrow. 'Name it, Banner.'

'Tell Cynthia Addleson I won't be makin' dinner tonight.'

'Will do. I s'pose I don't have to tell you to watch your back again?'

'Reckon you don't.'

'I can have a deputy stand outside tonight, if'n you're of a mind.'

'Won't be necessary, Marshal. Got all the protection I need.' He nudged his head at the Peacemaker on the chair.

'Suit yourself.' The marshal left and the doc followed him out, leaving Banner alone with his thoughts and the sinking notion Death had just taken a step closer to claim its due.

He drifted in and out of sleep, disturbed by occasional twinges of pain radiating from his ribs and snatches of nightmares drenched in blood. Faces whirled by: Jamie's, Cynthia's, Henkins's and Trombley's, along with the ghosts of men he had killed. The faces were distorted, gibbering, tainted by laudanum and guilt. Some became grinning skulls, blood streaking down their hollow-eyed faces. At times he struggled half from his sleep to hear vague noises in the outer office, but quickly sank back into the quicksand of his disturbed slumber after judging them to be non-threatening. He was conscious of the day darkening and the dusk settling in. Within the folds of encroaching night Jamie's ghostly figure formed, arms outstretched, beckoning, and he wanted desperately to go with her. He reached for her and she faded, his scream trailing into nothingness with her. A bright light formed, piercing his dreams, and within the glow danced the features of Jack Trombley, his bloody features accusing, a laugh ringing hollowly from his ragged lips. . . .

Banner awoke with a start and for an instant he thought the nightmare was real. Light surrounded him, blurred and buttery. His heart banged and he gasped, instinctively wanting to go for the gun on the chair.

'Luke?' a soft voice came.

He froze, unsure whether the voice came from somewhere in his dream.

You're slipping. . . .

'I'm so glad you're awake, Luke,' came the voice again. His vision sharpened and he realized the glow came from a lantern on a night table near by; he had not heard anyone enter the room, but knew someone must have done to light it. That gave him a stitch of dread, more so when he realized someone was sitting in a chair beside the bed. His vision focused on Cynthia Addleson's face. She had dragged a chair to his bedside and looked like an angel come to take his hand. He wondered how long she had been sitting there.

'Miss Cynthia . . .' he whispered, falling back into the bed.

She reached out and clasped his hand, smiling warmly. 'I'm glad you're all right, truly I am. I don't know what I would have done if you had been killed.'

'Marshal told you that, huh?'

She nodded, looking concerned. 'He wasn't going to, but I have a way of getting what I want.'

He smiled, mouth cottony and tongue thick. He caught a whiff of her perfume and it filled him with more comfort than any sawbones' opiate could have. 'How'd you get past the doc?'

She chuckled. 'Oh, he's a hard man, but you'd be surprised what a bit of feminine charm can do for a fella.'

Banner bet he wouldn't have been surprised at all, especially where a woman like Cynthia Addleson was concerned. She *was* an angel, least as far as he was involved, and the look of worry on her face gave him a strange sense of guilt, as if he had somehow nearly lost something dear to him. Again.

'Reckon you could charm the quills off a cactus, Miss Cynthia.'

She laughed, the sound intoxicating. 'Well, I don't know about that, but as I said I do generally find a way to get what I want. And right now I want you to get better, Luke. You owe me dinner and you're not getting out of it this easy.'

A smile came as easy as a cool stream on a summer day; it was a feeling he wasn't used to, at least not since Jamie died. 'Reckon I do at that.'

Her face turned serious as she appeared to struggle with some thought. Her sapphire eyes locked with his and he felt a shiver somewhere deep inside his soul, something melting, freeing itself, emotions he hadn't dared feel in so many years. 'It may not be my place to say this, Luke, but I've never cottoned to holdin' my tongue, least not in matters of importance. I've been lonely for a very long time, in fact, I never rightly thought there was more for me than opening my dress shop and living my life as a spinster.'

Lines deepened in Banner's brow. 'Don't see that, Miss Cynthia. You're a beautiful woman. Shorely many a man—'

'Oh, posh!' She held up her hand. 'Woods aren't nearly as full of them as you think, least not ones that are worth my time. You see after my raisin' going the way it did, I learned to stand on my own. Most men 'round these parts don't cotton to a strong woman who speaks her mind and I'm simply not the type to be attending church functions and ladies' socials. I can tell you more about a cattle ranch than most men and take a Winchester apart and put it back together with my eyes closed. I want a man who'll look at me as an equal and that attitude isn't exactly prevalent in the West.'

Banner chuckled. 'Ain't exactly prevalent anywhere, Miss Cynthia. Not in these times.'

She smiled and her hand went to her locket, fingering it absently. 'No, it is not. The East has its Victorian sensibilities and the West has its corset-cinched sense of skewed morality and bull-headed reasoning. Reckon I don't fit with neither of them.' She paused, as if turning over some thought, then looked back to him. 'Despite that, I am right tired of being alone, Luke. And until yesterday I was completely.'

'Till yesterday?' He didn't like where the conversation was heading, though something inside him desperately wanted it to stay on that trail. It was something else he could blame on the duplicity of Luke Banner, but it didn't make him a lick more comfortable.

'Until I met you, Luke. You're different from the rest of the men, here or back East. You're . . .'

(A killer. . . .)

Something passed over her eyes and again he could not put a peg to it, and the look vanished as soon as he tried. She smiled, though it came slightly strained. 'You're just not like other men.'

That was not what she intended to say, he felt sure, but it mattered little. He let out a scoffing grunt. 'No, Miss Cynthia, I ain't. Fact is, I ain't even sure what I am sometimes. I've spent so much of my life since . . . since Jamie died hunting down men who preyed on innocent folks. I reckon I lost whatever I was on that day she was murdered.'

A frown wandered over her lips and he knew instantly it was an expression he didn't like there. He liked her smiling, warm. A woman like Cynthia Addleson belonged full of life, happy, and he was a fool if he ever thought a man such as himself could do that for her.

'We have all lost folks . . .' Her voice came edged with a hint of coldness. 'Other people have taken things away from us and maybe you did more about that than most. I never had the option of confronting my brother's killer; maybe someday I will, but for now I go on and live with what happened, live despite what happened.'

'Reckon I don't catch your meanin'?'

She smiled and some of the warmth came back. 'You aren't living, Luke, it's plain to see. You spend your existence tracking men and never stop to really look where you've been, or where you are headed.'

Banner would have told most folks he was headed straight to Hell, but something about the seriousness in Cynthia Addleson's voice made him rein in his cynical nature. 'Don't see there's much choice for me at this point, Miss Cynthia. Been doin' what I've been doin' for too long.'

She shook her head. 'No, Luke. You got a choice. You don't want this any more, I can see it in your eyes every time you look at me. You want a life, now. You don't need to go after some Red Widow Gang and hardcases. You can start a new life somewhere – *we* can start a new life.'

A rush of emotion went through him, and he felt a strange cascade of feelings he had locked away since that day Jamie died. What she said was entirely inviting and when he looked into Cynthia Addleson's eyes he could almost see hope there, the chance for a new life, an end to the demon of revenge residing inside his soul.

Almost, but not quite.

She'll die just like Jamie if you love her, Banner. You know it. You can't let her take that risk.

Could he?

No. He could not.

'I gotta admit what you offer . . .' He paused, words locking in his throat. She squeezed his hand and he damn near said yes, they would ride off, start a new life together. He had enough money and it would be a simple matter of transferring funds to the account of an assumed name – in fact he kept a number of them set up for when he went in disguise on a case. They could buy a ranch and a few hundred head of cattle and . . .

No! He couldn't think that, couldn't let her risk her

life for a man who had for all intents died that day at the creek. He couldn't watch her die the way Jamie had.

'Luke, please. There's nothing for me in Arizona really. We can go somewhere and build ourselves a life, change our names and live away from everything we've been. Don't turn away from me. Let me help you forget the past; help me forget mine.'

The look in her eyes reached into his very soul, into the cold dark thing driving him, and somehow making all he had been want to fade into the shadows of the past and take all its ghosts with it.

Killer!

She leaned in and her lips touched his with the sensation of soft wings fluttering in his soul. He slid a hand behind her head, fingers sifting through her hair, his other hand gliding along her back. It had been so long since he had touched a woman and it was a sensation he had missed dearly, the feel of her soft bosom pressed against his chest and the scent of her perfume in his nostrils. He could get lost in that feeling, in her beauty and the sapphire seas of her eyes, let himself be free forever of the demon inside. His tongue found hers and he kissed her with a hunger brought by too many years without love and affection, only coldness and death.

You'll kill her, Banner, the same way you killed Jamie. The ghosts will come back and one of them will mean her death . . .

Nooo!

Something inside him screamed and then he was suddenly back at the creek, Jamie lying dead in his arms, her blood on his hands and on his soul. Then it was Cynthia's face staring sightlessly upwards, and a whirling confusion of images and guilt and darkness as the demon inside him struggled for life, struggled for dominance.

He pushed her away and the hurt look in her eyes pierced his soul. He averted his gaze, unable to look at her a moment longer or risk falling completely, knowing death came to a man in more ways than just a physical sense and he might have just died again.

'Luke, please . . .' she whispered. 'Don't do this. We can have a life together.'

'Please go, Miss Cynthia. I can't . . . I got a job to do, and an obligation.'

'An obligation?' Her voice came sharp and with an edge of accusation. She stood, anger flashing in her eyes. 'To whom? Some owner of a stage company you never agreed to work for in the first place? The faceless folks in towns who get their banks and stages robbed? You owe them nothing, Luke. They are nobody to you. You got your revenge. Just let the past be the past.'

He turned towards her, seeing a tear streaking down her cheek, and his conviction wavered. 'In all likelihood Zellers was killed 'cause he tried to hire me, Miss Cynthia. And someone called me to this town for a reason; I think that reason might just be to kill me. I can't risk your life, things bein' as they are.' As he said it his belly sank and he cursed himself for being a bigger fool than he had always thought himself to be. This woman before him was the only chance Luke Banner would have at living and he was sending her away.

'Taking that risk is for me to decide, Luke, not you. And I want to take it. I want to just disappear into the West and start a new life with you.'

His gaze narrowed. 'And what happens in a year, maybe more, maybe less, when you get lonesome for your sister and send her a telegram and someone

somehow links it to me? Or someone recognizes Luke
Banner from a pulp novel account and word gets out
and one night there's a man in our room with a gun, or
one in town who makes you a widow because I didn't
see a bullet coming from behind? I won't have that,
Miss Cynthia. I won't put you through another loss.
That *is* my choice.'

Another tear streaked from her eye and she turned,
hurrying towards the door. She gripped the edge and
looked back to him. 'I'm in love with you, Luke Banner.
And I think you're in love with me. Think about that
before you decide all the decisions are yours, because
they are not. Not when there are other folks involved.
You've seen enough death to know that by now.' She
spun and rushed through the door. He heard the outer
door slam. The doc peeked in and Banner waved him
away, wanting to be alone with his thoughts. He
wondered if he hadn't just made the biggest mistake of
his life, but his decision was made and that was that.
He was a stubborn old sonofabitch and maybe the
deathwish he'd always carried had just moved a step
closer towards fulfilling itself, for without Cynthia
Addleson in his life there was damn little left to live
for.

Luke Banner awoke from a restless sleep with a tingle
of apprehension. He lay in the darkened room, unmoving, eyes pressed shut and heart beating thickly. He
had drifted off to sleep shortly after Cynthia Addleson
left, plagued by guilt and dark regrets, the image of her
tear-streaked face, the ghost of her words. He had
never thought himself capable of feeling such things,
not since Jamie died, but sending her away had made
him long for a bottomless whiskey bottle. He had
settled for broken sleep.

Something had awoken him. What?

A sound, that was it. Barely perceived, more sensed, as if someone were sneaking up on his camp on a moonless night. A slight scuffing that might have escaped him had he been deeply asleep or still under the effects of the laudanum. He knew with all certainty someone was in the room with him, someone trying to make as little noise as possible.

Opening his eyes, he let his vision adjust to the gloom. Shreds of moonlight came through the blinds, providing scant illumination. He listened, holding his breath, barely able to hear above the muffled throbbing of his heart.

There!

The sound came again, a scuffing near the door. His gaze swung in that direction, though he didn't lift his head from the pillow or stir. He picked out the shadowy outline of a figure, though it appeared indistinct somehow, as if wearing loose clothing. The skulker was creeping towards him, choosing his steps carefully, and Banner caught a glint of moonlight flashing from metal.

The man had a gun!

That confirmed Banner's worst fears. Whoever had snuck into the room was here to finish the job previous attempts had failed at, and this time whoever it was wouldn't give the manhunter the chance to fight back.

Banner tensed, easing out the breath he'd been holding. His gaze flicked to the hardbacked chair beside the bed. With a quick roll he had a chance of getting his Peacemaker out of the holster before the skulker pulled the trigger. The bushwhacker didn't know he was awake and was making slow furtive movements towards the bed; if Banner could catch him by surprise. . . .

Another death, Banner. It's too dark to pick your shot

*and once you start the move you won't have time to aim
except to kill. . . .?*

He had no choice. It was a slim enough chance as it
was and the prowler would kill him if he didn't act.

Banner went for the gun. Without thought or hesitation he let instinct take over and twisted, hand dart-
ing out.

At the same instant the door burst open and a yell
stopped Banner short. A lantern threw buttery light
into the room and over the figure coming towards the
bed. The skulker was caught dead in the glare.

'What the hell's going on here?' came a shout and
with a sinking dread Banner knew the doctor had
come in to check on his patient and blundered into
something he was totally unprepared for.

The attacker was unprepared, too, but held a
distinct advantage. The figure whirled, panicked, and
jerked the trigger. A shot blasted, crashing like thunder in the confined area.

The doc stumbled backward, lantern flying from his
grip. Its chimney shattered as it hit the floor, kerosene
splashing out. With an explosive *whoof!* the fluid
ignited and flames streaked across the floor. The
figure, clearly outlined in the light, made a perfect
target and Banner didn't hesitate. He jerked his
Peacemaker free, swinging it around.

The attacker spun at the same time, endeavoring to
bring his gun to level on Banner.

Banner feathered the trigger and lead punched into
the fellow, kicking him backwards into the wall. His
finger spasmed on the trigger but the gun was aimed
at the floor and the bullet drilled into the hardwood.

The man crumpled, pitching forward and slamming
into the floor face first. Banner had no doubt the fellow
would not be getting up.

He pushed himself out of bed, body objecting, pain singing across his ribs. He fought to keep his balance, head spinning momentarily, legs weak.

Commotion came from the front as men piled into the office, the marshal leading them. The deputy grabbed a blanket and smothered the fire before it got out of hand. The room went dark and Banner fell back onto the bed, sitting on the edge, fighting a burst of nausea threatening to bring up the meal he'd picked at earlier.

The marshal located another lantern and lit it, illuminating the room. The lawdog went to the body of the attacker, holding the lantern over it and peering down. He shook his head. Banner looked over after getting his head to stop spinning. The killer, a hood obscuring his features, was dressed in black except for a red poncho draped over his shoulders.

Taking a deep breath, Banner stood, stronger this time. He glanced at the figure then at the marshal. The lawdog shifted his gaze to the manhunter. 'Reckon this ties the Red Widow Gang in with the reason you're here, Banner. No doubt of it now.'

Banner nodded. 'The doc?'

'Dead.' The marshal turned back to the figure. Scooching, he tugged the mask off the man, whom Banner recognized as the fellow who had pushed him through the rail earlier. If he had an inclination to go after the Red Widow Gang before it suddenly increased tenfold. They had come to him, revealed their hand, and he reckoned this case had a whole hell of a lot more behind it than he had figured on. The attempt on his life was clear this time and deathwish aside, he didn't want to provide them with another opportunity of burying him.

SEVEN

'Half the town will be dead 'fore you get through, Banner.' A grim expression crossed Marshal Hart's features and Luke Banner, sitting in the hardbacked chair reckoned he couldn't rightly blame him. He had brought nothing but death and violence to Bellstar since arriving, but for the life of him he couldn't tell why.

Banner stared into the shafts of morning sunlight arcing through the dusty window panes, watching dust minuet within, his mind wandering.

The Red Widow Gang. Zellers had been killed shortly after trying to hire him to chase them down, but that might still have been coincidence, though a goddamn unlikely one. The attack last night clinched one thing: the gang did not want Banner on the case and had made a direct attempt to prevent that by sending a killer to the doc's. Was that related to the other attacks? Banner was becoming more and more certain of it. The man last night had been with the hardcase named Henkins at Zellers' nephew's house, and Henkins had been involved in the attack on Cynthia in the alley. A tenuous link had formed; Banner bet if he kept digging that link would get a whole lot stronger.

Had the gang lured him to Bellstar?

He wondered. Someone had, but so far no one had stepped forward and Zellers claimed not to be the one. Banner believed him. Someone else had brought him here and the attacks, however well disguised, had begun shortly thereafter. It made little sense, yet it had to have a connection.

Why would that gang want him dead? Because of his reputation? He doubted it. He posed no threat to them as long as he was not on the case, and to bring him here invited the opportunity for a man like Zellers to hire him. If they had lured him here based on the off-chance he would hear about the gang and take the case, they had unwittingly brought it about themselves; Banner didn't think a gang as crafty as the Red Widows were likely to do that.

No, Banner felt sure it was something else, some other reason, something he was overlooking, or completely unaware of.

He shifted in the chair, ribs aching and body stiff, though better than the previous night. 'The Red Widow Gang wants me dead, Marshal. I'd like to know why now.'

The marshal nodded. 'Thought occurred to me, too, but I ain't quite sure why they'd want that, either.' The lawdog peered at Banner, as if studying him.

'Somethin' on your mind, Marshal?' Banner asked, seeing a question behind the man's eyes.

The marshal shook his head, but Banner wasn't convinced. 'Reckon not, 'cept right now I'm kinda wonderin' why exactly you're alive.'

Banner let out a grunt. 'Been in this line of work too long to sleep any deeper than a cat does, Marshal. Reckon it don't take much to alert me to the fact someone's sneakin' up on me.'

The marshal's brow crinkled, deep worry lines looking like little rivers. 'Ain't what I mean and you know it.'

'Reckon you best lay it on the table, then.'

'You got a death wish, Banner. It's plain to see. Yet there's somethin' else, somethin' contradictory, I reckon. You want to die, yet you don't.'

Banner felt himself tense; the marshal had hit the nail on the head. He doubted he could explain it himself, but for some godforsaken reason something inside him had kept him alive all these years, despite the situations he seemed to deliberately maneuver himself into. He didn't know what it was, only that it existed and that had become even more plain the other night when he couldn't pull the trigger of the gun pressed to his temple.

You're a Janus, Banner, pure and simple.

That might be true and maybe he'd never really understand it. He only knew it had gotten stronger since meeting Cynthia Addleson.

'Might be right, Marshal. Sometimes . . .' Banner's eyes clouded and for a moment he felt lost somewhere inside himself. 'Sometimes I wish – *pray* that some hardcase's bullet will find me. Put an end to the thing I've become. That all the ghosts of the men I've killed will stop haunting me because I'll be with them and they'll finally be satisfied.' Banner pressed his eyes shut, thoughts wandering to Trombley and the fight in the saloon. Reopening them, he took a deep breath. 'But then I just keep fightin' it. I don't let them win and maybe I *can't* let them win till it's by their skill and not by something I've held back.'

The marshal laughed, a sound devoid of humor and almost mocking. 'That's because you ain't a thing, Banner. You're a man, flesh and bone like me, like anyone, maybe just touched by the Devil though God knows you likely didn't ask for it. I seen plenty of manhunters in my time. You're different. The same thing don't drive you as drives them. Some do it for money and are little better than the men they track down. Just glorified hardcases with an itchy trigger and horse sense enough to cloak themselves in some questionable guise of law.'

'The rest?' Banner cocked an eyebrow.

'They do it for duty. They got a notion they're makin' the West a better place, that maybe they can play God just a bit and clean the almighty Devil's handiwork from the Maker's earth. Often as not they get disillusioned 'cause it never stops. One hardcase dies, two more spring up to take his place. First bunch, well, they lose control, maybe kill under just the wrong circumstances and get their necks stretched, or get too damn fool-headed to know when to stop and a faster gun puts them in Boot Hill. Don't really matter.'

Banner's face pinched. 'And me, Marshal?'

'Like I said, you're different. You got some demon drivin' you, but you're tired, too. I see it in your eyes, and I see it more when you speak Cynthia Addleson's name. You got a death wish but you also got a life wish, 'cept maybe you'll suffer the same end them first fellas who don't see the end comin' do.'

'You're sayin' I'll get myself killed?'

'Damn straight! Look at you. Trombley damn near put a bullet in ya and from what you told me, the hardcase with the knife came close, too. Then Henkins and his partner damn near killed you at Zellers' nephew's place. Last night the Red Widow Gang might've succeeded but for the doc and some sixth sense you still got functioning. You ever got this stove up before?' The marshal drilled him and Banner knew the man was right. His last case had gotten him more bruises than he would have liked and this one more than matched that. The two combined 'bout equaled everything in his career.

He sighed, wanting to deny the truth. 'Reckon I got another case or two in me, Marshal,' he said, despite himself, knowing damn well the fool who didn't admit he was going over the hill woke up one day to find himself at the bottom of it.

The marshal scoffed, folding his arms and leaning back in his chair. 'Reckon I'll be findin' *your* body next, Banner, and it won't be all that long from now. Then whatever evil rode into this town will ride out all the more smug and singin' to its lonesome and that will be that. Bellstar will go on way it did before, maybe even a bit more weary than it is.'

He's right, Banner. Your time's been comin' for a spell now and you've borrowed everything left to lend. Give it up and disappear into the pulp novels. Don't be a fool any more than you've already been.

'What about you, Marshal? Will you go on the same as these folks?' Banner ducked his chin towards the door.

'Me? Hell, I'll just be left with a goddamn bitter taste in my mouth. I'm too old to be chasin' down Red Widow bandits on my own and I know it. I've had my share of call-outs and cow thieves. Now I just keep the peace and damn little ever interrupts that—'

'Leastwise till I came along.' A cynical edge honed Banner's voice.

The marshal nodded. 'Leastwise.'

Banner stood, going to the window and gazing out into the sunlit street, watching passers-by scurry about their business, past tragedies having wiped all compassion and neighborly goodwill from their faces.

They focused on what they had in mind and paid no attention to anything or anyone other than that.

'You may have no choice, Marshal. This gang has come to Bellstar. You won't just sit there while they run through it like the Culverins did. I see that in *your* eyes.' He turned and gazed at the marshal and the lawdog nodded slowly.

'Then I'll do what I have to do, but I'll do it with every hope that I come out alive and kickin'.'

'You might get your chance, Marshal, and you can make those odds a little better than they will be if you just sit here waitin' for the Devil to pay you a visit.'

The marshal cocked an eyebrow, face going a shade darker. 'You're goin' after 'em, ain't you?'

Banner laughed without humor. 'Reckon I got a notion to. They made it personal last night when they tried to kill me. I don't cotton to that. But I know this gang's been causing enough hell to make them probably the most dangerous bunch I've gone after and I reckon I'm admittin' maybe I could use some help.'

'Oh, Christamighty, Banner. . . .' The marshal let out a long sigh and his lips drew into a tight line.

Banner grinned. 'You ain't quite ready for pasture yet, either, Marshal, despite your talk.'

Marshal Hart shook his head slowly, but a thin smile played on his lips. 'Reckon I'm a hell of a fella to be dolin' out advice, then.'

Banner cocked his head and turned back to the window. 'Ain't many folks I let myself get close to, Marshal. Most who hire me go on about their lives when the deed's done, heedless of the blood on their own hands. Others, they either see me as a butcher or look at me with the same kind of fear you give a rabid coyote. It don't matter none, really, it just is.'

'Ain't sure I catch your meanin', Banner.'

Luke Banner folded his arms and took a breath. 'Ain't many a man I count as friend, Marshal. Reckon I would you, though. Least as much as a man like me ever could.'

The marshal glanced at his desktop then back to Banner. 'That's a right high honor comin' from a man like you. And I reckon you're right on the mark. Seein' you makes me wish I was still a young pup lookin' to put justice into the West. Maybe I'll get my damn fool head shot off but I figure you're right and I will anyway if I sit around waitin'. You got my respect and you got my friendship. And you got my help in whatever you want to do.'

Banner turned, nodding. 'Much obliged, Marshal.'

'Don't thank me for sendin' you to your death, and maybe bringin' on my own.'

Banner chuckled. 'You ain't sendin' me. I'm ridin' into this free will.' Banner paused, a somber feeling washing over him. Something inside had changed, something subtle, and maybe last night when Cynthia had come to his room at the doc's she had made it all the more clear. This had to be his last case, one way or the other, by bullet or by banishment.

He wondered if the choice would really be his.

Whatever the case, a man named Luke Banner would die.

'We need a place to start, Banner. We can't just go askin' around where they hide out, and they wear them get-ups for a reason.'

'Reckon it lets 'em walk around right under everyone's nose without a care.' Banner's brow furrowed. 'That man last night, you seen him around before he attacked me?'

The marshal shook his head. 'Not till I saw him scoot from the back of the house yesterday. Looked through some Wanted posters earlier, though, and he's got a record long as a spinster's skirt.'

'Who was he?'

'Man name of Jasper Cruz. Comes from a town up Wyoming way called Dawson Pass.'

A look of shock hit Banner's face and a flash of memory thundered through his mind. In a flash of violent images, he relived the day Jamie died by the creek and then a night where he had tracked her murderer's boss to his home and killed him, leaving him in a well for 'hands to discover.

'Banner?' he heard the marshal ask distantly. He shook his head and his gaze focused on the lawdog, who was peering at him intently. 'What is it? You know him?'

Banner shook his head. 'No, not exactly. But I know the town he comes from. Brings back . . . a time I ain't partial to recollectin'. Man who hired Jamie's killers came from that town.'

'Jamie?' The marshal cocked an eyebrow.

'Someone . . . I loved.' Banner felt sadness burn in his heart. 'We were to be married. She was killed because this man wanted some land I won bid on.'

Marshal shook his head. 'Hell of a thing.'

'Reckon it is. Funny the price some folks put on things. Wants get more precious than life and next thing you know you're paying the devil.'

'You think there's a connection?'

Banner shrugged. 'Might be just a coincidence but there's a hell of a lot of those going around lately.'

'I'm inclined to agree.'

Banner's thoughts started to wander back to that time but then he forced them away. He didn't need to think of that now. It would only make things worse. If there was link somehow he would find it. If not, then it was just a callous God's idea of a joke and he'd damn well had enough of them.

He peered at the marshal. 'Zellers' stage still runnin' tomorrow?'

The marshal nodded. 'Far as I know. Nephew's taken over the company till everything can be tended to legal-like. Zellers had family but all of 'em 'cept the nephew were scattered across the country. Reckon they'll be like vultures on a corpse soon as they get word. Man like that usually gets what he gives.'

Banner agreed. 'I want to be on that stage.'

Shock hit the marshal's features. 'You ain't serious?'

'Dead serious. Zellers himself suggested it. There'll be four other guards, all armed, two drivin' the stage and two inside. That's the way it runs. You and your deputy will ride maybe a mile back and keep inconspicuous just in case. I need to know what kind of pattern the gang uses for their robberies, too.'

The marshal shook his head. 'You *do* have a death wish.'

Luke Banner grinned, but felt far from confident. He was placing himself in a hell of a position, one he normally didn't risk. He preferred tracking down hardcases, one on one encounters, and damn few ever saw the end of a rope. This . . . this was different, perhaps suicidal. He would be smack in the middle of the ambush and lead would be flying every which way.

The marshal sighed. 'They usually strike hard and fast, use dynamite sometimes to stop the stage; other times they just surround it and kill all aboard.'

Banner had to admit that could prove potentially problematic. The gang had pulled off their robberies with deadly precision so far, but maybe this time they wouldn't have the element of surprise on their side. All aboard knew the stage was likely to be hit, would be prepared, and Banner would have three men – the marshal, deputy and guard he replaced who normally rode in the stage – pulling drag. The gang would not expect that.

'How many of 'em?'

The marshal shrugged. 'Hard to say. Least four by accounts. Maybe more, maybe less. An' you killed at least one of 'em.'

'Replacements will be waitin' in the wings, Marshal. Always are. Be better if we knew for certain, but plan for more.'

'Stage should come through 'round noon. I'll check with the nephew and git all the details. Meet me here tomorrow morning, six sharp, and we'll go over the specifics.'

Banner nodded and the somber feeling inside him grew stronger. Noon tomorrow at the latest. He wondered if he would see another sundown and suddenly more doubt crept in than he would have liked.

You are getting old. . . .

He got little time to ponder the thought, because a shot sounded and the window suddenly imploded in a shimmering rain of spiralling glass. The bullet drove into the floor, missing Banner by fractions of an inch.

From the street came screams and the frantic clomping of boots running down the boardwalk, as townsfolk dashed for their homes or bolted into shops.

With the shot Banner dived to the floor. A second shot nipped at the heels of the first. He heard a shriek of lead and a bullet buried itself in the floor where he had been standing.

The marshal let out a curse and hunkered down behind his desk, drawing his Colt.

Banner slid his gun free and flattened himself

against the wall to the left of the shattered window.

A hush fell and all he heard was the muffled pounding of his heart. He looked over to see the marshal crawling on hands and knees, gun in hand, towards the window. The lawdog positioned himself to Banner's right, on the other side of it.

'Judas H. Priest, Banner. I was expectin' gunplay, but I thought it might hold off till we were with the stage at least. You're damn lucky whoever's firin' missed you.'

Banner shook his head. 'No luck involved. Whoever fired that shot missed me on purpose. It was a warning.'

'Hell's bells! Why would anyone warn you after tryin' to kill you last night? Don't make no sense.'

Banner had to admit he didn't understand it either. Someone wanted him dead, that was clear, had called him to Bellstar for just that purpose and likely arranged numerous attempts to that end. Yet with his back to the window, presenting a clear target, they had either suddenly developed damn poor aim or purposely missed, and he felt certain it was the latter.

He waited, no sound coming from the street. The shots had cleared the townsfolk and there was only an eerie silence. He eased upward, cautiously peering out through the window, careful not to show himself. As he expected, the street was deserted. His gaze jumped from building to building. From the angle of the second bullet he laid bet whoever had fired was poised atop a roof, shooting downward.

There!

On a rooftop on the opposite side of the street, he caught a glint of sunlight reflecting off a rifle barrel. Squinting, he saw a crouched figure, dressed in black and red.

'Looks like the Red Widow Gang is here to stay after all, Marshal.' He gazed at the lawman. 'One of 'em's shootin' at me.'

The marshal's face twisted with a perplexed look. 'The Red Widow Gang shootin' to miss? Ain't god-damned likely.'

It made damn little sense to Banner as well, but right now he didn't rightly care. He shoved his Peacemaker through the opening, resting the barrel on the sill. He aimed for where he had seen the glint of metal.

The figure must have seen sunlight glint from Banner's own barrel for another shot blasted immediately. The bullet ploughed into the windowsill, splintering it just where Banner's Peacemaker was resting, confirming whoever was shooting was an expert marksman who should not have missed.

Banner jerked his gun back then jabbed it forward, readjusting his aim, and triggered off a hasty shot.

He missed but heard the sudden clomping of boots as the bushwhacker retreated. The marshal leaned over and triggered a shot of his own, but came nowhere close to the Red Widow bandit.

Banner vaulted to his feet, going for the door. The marshal followed suit, only a couple of beats behind.

Pressing close to the door, he eased it open, and peered out. He saw the figure leap the gap to an adjacent building, lithe as a cat, and pumped a hasty shot in that direction, knowing he'd never hit the bandit. Expectedly, the shot fell far short and Banner knew by the time he reached the rooftop the bandit would be long gone.

He stepped outside, staring in that direction, wondering why the attacker, obviously a member of the Red Widow Gang, had chosen to miss after other attempts on his life. He glanced at the marshal, who peered at him then at the rooftop.

'Six tomorrow, Banner,' he said, a slight hitch in his voice. 'I'd recommend you don't stand in front of any windows till that time.'

Banner nodded, but something inside told him the reason for that miss was far more complicated than he could fathom without a lot more pieces of the puzzle, and that there would not likely be another attempt on his life until he was nestled aboard a stage riding straight into the lead hellfire of an ambush tomorrow.

EIGHT

By the time Banner clambered his way onto the rooftop from which the attack had come, the bushwhacker was long gone. He'd spent half an hour searching, and discovered nothing to indicate anyone had ever been there. That left him with nothing but a saddle-bag full of questions and a dull banging in his skull.

He took a deep breath and his brow furrowed. He'd been thinking on it half the day and as he sauntered along the boardwalk, the day withering and dusk making shadows long and reaching, he felt no closer to putting together a reason for the events that had transpired since his arrival in Bellstar. A mysterious someone had hired him, a deposit of considerable amount transferred to an agency account. The money had been wired from Bellstar, though the bank man only vaguely recollected a man had ordered the transaction. From the description given, Banner now figured that man to be the hardcase from the alley, Henkins.

So far no one but Zellers had contacted him, though the stage owner denied calling the manhunter to Bellstar. Banner believed him. The man had no reason to lie and now the stage owner was dead after trying to hire his services. Yet how would anyone have known the man wanted to engage him?

Banner reckoned he knew: Zellers likely made no secret of his presence in town. At some point the man had mentioned his intentions to hire a manhunter to track the Red Widow Gang and that had gotten him killed. The more Banner thought about it the more he figured those killers had not expected him to show up at the nephew's homestead. They were likely as surprised to see the manhunter as he was them.

He had other pieces, though they made about as much sense. Trombley had drawn him into the fight on purpose and the hardcases had grabbed Cynthia off the street to lure him into the alley. Yet, something about those attacks didn't correspond to the one at the doc's office. Until that point the Red Widow Gang had gone to great lengths to keep themselves from being associated with the attempts, make them appear to be random incidents. The attack in the doc's office was different; it directly linked the bandits to the reason Banner was in town. Why suddenly come out into the open that way?

And why shoot at him from a rooftop and deliberately miss?

Because the attacker wanted to warn him off the case? He doubted it. They were assuming he would take it, maybe because of the hardcase killed at the doc's and Banner's presence at the marshal's. So why not kill him and assure themselves he would not cause trouble? Isn't that what they had brought him to Bellstar to do anyway?

The more he chewed it over the more the pieces didn't fit and the more his skull ached. He gave up on the thoughts for the time being. Maybe tomorrow he would have his answers, when he rode that stage laden with gold. For now he had other things to occupy his mind.

He sighed, a twinge of pain bedeviling his ribs, thoughts turning towards his conversation with the marshal. The lawdog accused Banner of looking tired, worn, carrying a death wish, yet a life wish as well. Maybe Hart was dead right. If that weren't the case Banner reckoned he would have seen a bone orchard years ago, and wouldn't have made it past the gun barrel jammed to his temple the other night.

But where did that leave him?

With a last case – chase down the Red Widow Gang and discover the reason they had brought him here to kill him.

Simple enough motivation, yet perhaps a deadly execution of plan. Place himself on that stage tomorrow, in the direct line of the bandits' attack and risk everything. Make that last draw and pray the other gunfighter wasn't just a shade quicker than a slipping manhunter.

As the dusk deepened and shadows grew thicker, Luke Banner stopped across from the hotel, peering for long moments at the door. He had done a lot of pondering after that shot missed him this morning, on the marshal's words, and on his own confused motivations and feelings. Cynthia Addleson was a hell of a lot more responsible for bringing that to a head than he had wanted to admit. After Jamie died, he had become a thing of vengeance and cold retribution. He had survived that way for countless empty nights, courting death, letting it creep just so close and perhaps wishing for its victory. But now. . . ?

Now he had to admit it was all turned upside down and maybe he'd never outrun the ghosts, but maybe somehow he could find a way to live with them.

Live. No longer survive, exist for vengeance. Live a life where maybe the few dreams he and Jamie planned could be brought to bear and in some small way honor her with more than just an endless string of bloody bodies.

Jamie would prefer that to what he had become and he reckoned it was something he had always known, though refused to accept. How could he? When he blamed himself for failing to save her, failing to see past his own desire for a life with her to realize he had attracted a certain danger by bidding against a man who was little better than a common hardcase. He hadn't seen then, hadn't been the thing of dark suspicion and hardened emotion he was now. Perhaps it wouldn't have mattered anyway, because he'd been too young and impetuous at the time and nothing could have swayed his course. The guilt would never leave, though he knew Jamie would never have wanted him to carry the dread responsibility of her death. She would never have blamed him and would want him to go on with his life. And perhaps with Cynthia there was at least that chance.

For the first time since Jamie's death he felt a desire to live, a need to shed the dark thing inside him, bury the demon.

He had stopped by the bank and conducted a transaction that placed $100,000 from his accounts into that of a man named Brett Drake, a name he had saved as a ruse in case needed, a man who as of this moment did not exist. When he brought down the Red Widow Gang – it he brought them down – Luke Banner would cease to exist and Brett Drake would spring full grown from the loins of greenbacks and gold and unfulfilled dreams. He would buy a small ranch somewhere up Montana way, but before that he would ask Cynthia to join him.

That decision came with a risk, of course, and he

might never truly stop looking over his shoulder and sitting with his back to the wall. But he would take that gamble. One way or the other Luke Banner would die tomorrow. And for the first time in an eternity he found himself hoping it was not by a bandit's bullet.

He had attended to other details as well. At the telegraph office he sent a message to his personal secretary, instructing him to shut down the agency and set loose employees with a year's wages. He told the secretary to take five years' wages and report that Luke Banner had vanished on a case and never come back. He had paid the telegraph operator handsomely to let him tap out the message himself and instructed the secretary to destroy all traces of anything pertaining to it and to his coming to Bellstar.

It would not be enough, but he would make more arrangements in secret, leave blind trails and false leads to his vanishing and he hoped that would make the difference. He had the means to live a comfortable life and if Cynthia wanted to join him he reckoned he would have something as close to happiness as a man like Luke Banner could ever be allowed.

Upon departing the telegraph office he had wandered into the small white church at the edge of town. A first for a man who'd never taken any comfort in religion, considered himself as far removed from his God as a man could be. There he knelt before the altar and prayed. Prayed for every man he had ever killed and every ghost that haunted him, and prayed Jamie would forgive him for letting feelings for another woman warm his thoughts. He knew she would and likely wherever she was already had, but he needed to ask and make his peace and that was something Luke Banner had put off for far too long.

His gaze focused again on the hotel and he drew a deep breath.

You may be her death, Banner, if you come through tomorrow. She may end up like Jamie and you will be responsible again. You'll have more innocent blood on your hands, Do you really want that?

That was possible and he felt great dread course through him at the notion. But it was different now, too. Despite the subtle and not so subtle signs of slippage, he was a far different man than he had been when Jamie was killed. He had honed certain skills of self-preservation to a keen edge and maybe that would prevent events from repeating themselves. He found himself clinging to that tenuous hope.

Do you love her?

He reckoned he did, though she would never replace Jamie and that was the only way for it to be. For now that was all he could offer and Cynthia would know it. The choice would be hers and it was asking a lot. But it was the best he could do.

He walked across the street and entered the hotel. The clerk glanced up then promptly ignored him, going back to reading his pulp novel. Banner climbed the stairs and made his way to Cynthia's room, stopping just outside the door, heart beating a tick faster.

He knocked and from within the room came vague sounds of someone coming towards the door.

'Who is it?' he heard her ask and the sound of her voice sent shivers of emotion through him. He felt awkward yet strangely content with the feelings.

'It's me, Miss Cynthia: Luke Banner.'

The door opened and his eyes met hers. An expression of surprise and joy warmed her features. She wore a blouse and jeans and he reckoned she looked just as lovely in those as a fancy dress. Waiting, she peered at him expectantly and he removed his hat, glancing at the floor, then back up.

'I've been thinkin' about what you said, Miss Cynthia, and I reckon if you'll still have me I'd like to give it a try. Best be warned it won't be easy and we'll be lookin' back more times than we'll be lookin' forward, but I can offer you some comforts and you'll never want for anything.'

She smiled and touched his hand. 'I just want a life, Luke. I don't want to go to sleep at night wishing my arms were full and wakin' up in an empty bed with nothing to look forward to but going to my dress shop and pretending that fills every hole in my life. It don't, not by a long sight. You got something inside you I never expected to see and I've fallen in love with you, Luke Banner. I've taken care of myself for a long time. I can handle anything that comes our way and I accept what you're offerin'.'

He let a thin smile turn his lips. 'I ain't so sure you might not think different the first time someone takes a shot at one of us, but maybe it won't happen.'

She let out a glassy laugh. 'I got a notion anyone who takes a shot at us will be in for a bad time. My brother didn't skimp in teachin' me the ways of the West. Reckon you'll find I'm a good bit more sturdy than you're thinking.'

'Reckon I will at that.' He pulled her into his arms and kissed her deeply, a fire of passion surging through his body. He kissed her with all the pent-up intensity the years of emptiness had laid upon him. She drew him into the room and he kicked the door shut behind them. Gazing into her eyes he unpinned her hair, letting it fall across her shoulders like spun gold caught by a gentle wind. His fingers traveled along her blouse, unbuttoning each button with building anticipation. He hadn't been with a woman for so long, and he reckoned the doves he had spent time with hardly counted. Their practiced pleasures and bought whispers could never compare to the feelings Cynthia Addleson brought out in him, and as he dwelled on it he realized just how empty it had been. He had never been with Jamie in the Biblical way, and it was something he regretted almost every moment of his life. That would not happen again.

He slipped the blouse from her shoulders, exposing the camisole beneath. She undid his shirt and let it fall to the floor. Her fingers went to his gun belt, hesitated an instant, then unhooked the buckle. He caught the belt and hung it over the corner of the bed and a strange sense of freedom came with it.

As she lifted her arms, he drew the camisole over her head, exposing her beauty. He reckoned he had never seen a sight so lovely. The locket hung at her neck, catching glints of dying light from a window. He lifted her and carried her to the bed, laying her gently atop the covers and letting himself drown within the depths of her sapphire eyes.

The dream came again.

The nightmare.

After making love to Cynthia Addleson, knowing the greatest happiness he had felt since before Jamie died, he had held her in his arms until he heard the gentle rhythm of her breath indicate she had fallen asleep. Then he had let himself drift off, the warmth of emotion and passion still aglow within him.

He was suddenly awake, gazing into Jamie's eyes. Sunlight streamed through her golden hair, framing her lovely face. Her features melted away, becoming a skull, a grinning vile thing that stared with depthless black sockets and laughed with the hollow mirth of Death. It mocked him, telling him he was not entitled to the feelings of warmth and satisfaction he found tonight, that there was only darkness and emptiness and death for a man who had killed and killed, for a man who was not a man at all, but a machine of vengeance and retribution.

You can't escape what you are, Banner. You can never escape!

Then Jamie's face formed again and the hardcases who had attacked them that fateful day stepped from the bushes.

The thunder of shots, echoing from the past, shuddering through his mind.

He lunged for the hardcase, as he had in a thousand empty nightmares. A whirling of images, distorted and frantic. The man's gun blasting, Jamie's shriek, the cry that reverberated through every moment of every hour of every day since she died, never stopping, simply embedding itself into his guilty soul until he wanted to come apart.

He killed the man. Again. As he always did. That never changed. And it always came too late to save her.

When he turned she lay there, eyes vacant and staring sightlessly upward.

And blood. So much blood. Streaming through his hands as he cradled her in his arms.

You killed me, Luke. . . .

Her lips seemed to move, accusing him, though that couldn't possibly be with her lifeblood soaking into the Wyoming ground.

And you'll kill her. . . .

'Nooo!'

A scream tore from his throat and he sat bolt upright, heart hammering, sweat pouring down his face. His breath beat out in ragged gasps. For a moment he saw Jamie's blood-stained face in the darkness, but it quickly vanished, an after-effect of the nightmare. He put his face in his hands, deep sobs wracking his body.

A hand gently touched his shoulder and he lifted his face from his hands and saw Cynthia beside him, heedless of her nakedness as she clutched to him, holding him in the throbbing gloom of the hotel room.

'It's all right, Luke. It was only a dream.'

He uttered a humorless laugh and drew a deep breath, trying to regain his composure. 'I keep reliving the day she died. It always ends the same and tortures me, Miss Cynthia. I reckon I'll never be rid of it.'

Touching his cheek, she peered into his eyes. 'You don't have to, Luke. I'll always be here when you wake up with it. And it won't happen with us. I promise you that. There are things. . . .' She hesitated, as if she were struggling with something inside her she couldn't quite put words to. 'There are things we can do to make sure it never happens again. Please believe me.'

For the second time he got the notion she intended to say something else, but it didn't matter because he did believe her. Something in her voice told him Cynthia Addleson had survived more than she had told and was one hell of a strong woman. What had happened with Jamie would never happen with her.

'I do, Miss Cynthia. I reckon I'll always be haunted by what happened to her and by all the men I've killed. There's no escape from that.'

She stared off into the darkness and her words came out almost a whisper. 'Reckon I will too, Luke. Was a time I thought ghosts could be chased down, dealt with. Then all past wrongs would be wiped clean from the earth and from my memory. But things don't always go the way a body expects them to. I'm not much different from you, Luke. For a while I had a notion I might find my brother's killer and make him pay for what he did. I carried that thought around far too long and it damn near chewed me up inside. It changed me and made me into something I didn't want to be. Now everything is . . . *different*. I don't want the ghosts any more than you want yours, but we got no choice because they ain't just gonna leave. I reckon maybe that's OK because what we have will be strong enough to keep them away some, or at least make them tolerable.'

She turned her head back to him and he gazed at her, his fingers lifting to caress her cheek. Something in her voice made him want to hold her, comfort her, remove all the pain she had suffered, but how could he when he couldn't even remove his own?

'I ain't sure they're so willin' to be tolerated, Miss Cynthia.'

She gave a low laugh and smiled. 'Let's go away, tonight, or least at first light. I want to be as far away from Colorado as possible this time tomorrow. I want to be started on our new life and never look back on what was.'

A mixture of dread and guilt rose in his heart. He hadn't told her his plans to leave at false dawn to meet the marshal and arrange to meet the stage coming in tomorrow. Now he had no choice.

'I can't, Miss Cynthia. Make no mistake I want to, but I can't leave yet. . . .'

She peered at him, face registering confusion. 'I don't understand. Nothing's holding us here, now. We can just ride out and never look back. You told me you had it all arranged.'

He felt his belly sink and let out a long sigh. 'There's

a stage coming in tomorrow carryin' a shipment of gold. The one Zellers told us about that day at the café. I plan to be on it.'

Shock hit her face and her eyes widened. Her mouth came open, then closed and hard lines creased her face. He saw fear mix with the shock in her eyes. She shook her head. 'No, Luke. You can't. You'll get yourself killed. You can't do that to me.'

'Got no choice, Miss Cynthia. The Red Widow Gang tried to kill me. I reckon they brought me here for that reason, though I can't tell you I know why or understand the way they're going about it. I just know I won't leave a loose end that might somehow follow us. When that stage is attacked I will be on it and put an end to the Red Widow Gang. There's no other way.'

'Please, Luke, don't.' Her voice came low and with a sense of grimness and pain he could hardly bear. 'You don't have to do this. That gang has killed everyone they've come across, way I heard it told and you'll give them no choice but to kill you, too.'

'I do have to do it, Miss Cynthia. I have to finish things or I can't start over.'

'You'll die . . .' she whispered, turning away from him and settling back, hand on her chest.

He eased himself back down and lay staring up at the ceiling, knowing she might well be right and unable to promise her any different.

'God willing, I'll come back, Miss Cynthia and we'll leave first light the next day.'

'You won't come back, Luke,' she said with a hardness in her voice that showed deep pain. 'You'll get yourself killed and I'll be alone again. We got a choice tonight but it won't be there tomorrow. There's no way to stop those bandits from striking and killing. But we can stop them from killing you and our chance at happiness if we leave now.'

He wanted to leave with her, ride as far and as fast away from Bellstar and the past as he possibly could. With everything inside him he wanted to. But couldn't. If he didn't finish this he didn't put an end to the man Luke Banner was and give the one he would become the chance at living.

'I have to, Miss Cynthia. There's no other way. I can't explain it any more than that.'

She remained silent and they lay there until false dawn spread grey across the sky. As dusky light bled through the windows he dressed and strapped on his gunbelt, the iron feeling heavier than it had ever felt in his life. He paused at the door, and turned back to her and she didn't look at him. 'I . . .' he started, not sure what to say.

'Don't say anything, Luke, unless it's I love you. I don't want to recollect anything else when you don't come back.'

'I do love you, Miss Cynthia. It's the only thing I'm sure of right now.'

He slowly turned the handle and opened the door, stepping out and closing it gently behind him. He hoped he wasn't closing it on the only thing that meant a damn to him in an eternity of lonely years.

NINE

Dusty shafts of mid-morning sunlight arced through the branches of ponderosa pine, blue spruce and flutter-leafed aspens and fell across the rutted trail in indistinct patches. A whispering breeze shushed through the leaves and boughs. The sky carried a gauzy haze, making it look milky sapphire. A hawk glided above and lark buntings chittered away.

Luke Banner and Marshal Hart sat their horses to the left of the trail, on a wooded upraise. Behind them a creek snaked through the countryside, uttering trickling whispers.

A tense expression tightened Banner's face. He felt anything but comfortable about the prospect of what lay ahead. The gold-laden stage would rattle through within the hour and they would meet up with it. One of the guards would take Banner's horse while he, exchanging places, climbed aboard the stage. Two guards would be driving and another would accompany Banner inside the cab. The marshal and other guard, along with a deputy, would ride a mile or so back.

Despite the danger involved, he found his thoughts locked on one image – the sight of Cynthia Addleson as he left her in the hotel room. He had cursed and second-guessed himself from the moment he walked out the door. He promised to come back, but could he really tell her that in all good faith with such a high risk involved? He reckoned it didn't make much difference, because if something went wrong he'd never have to answer for it.

He had given her his excuses, that he needed to tie this up so no loose ends would hunt them down and ruin any chance of happiness they had and that was the God's honest truth as he saw it. But what if there was another way? What if they had just left and disappeared? Would the Red Widow Gang bother to come after him?

He supposed that in order to determine that he needed to know why they were after him in the first place. That answer might be provided shortly.

'You got the look of a man worryin' a notion, Banner,' came the voice of the marshal.

Banner's gaze focused on the man next to him leaning a forearm on the pommel and peering at him with concern and curiosity. 'Ever wonder 'bout a decision you made, knowin' it was right but knowin' you might be sacrificing somethin' more important?'

The lawdog shrugged, cocking his head. 'Reckon maybe a few times. But a man like you . . . man like you knows his gut, Banner, 'cept maybe where quittin' is concerned.'

Banner lifted his hat and with his bandanna wiped a film of sweat from his forehead. He could have told the marshal in no uncertain terms this was his last case, that after today Luke Banner would fade into the pulp novels and good riddance to him. But he didn't. Because a somber uneasiness had wandered over him and he couldn't put a finger to it. Maybe it was that sixth sense of danger again – though he didn't rightly need that to tell him what he was doing might get him buried – or maybe it was simply a gunfighter getting too damn old to know the difference, but a sudden overwhelming notion told him things might be heading for a showdown that would present him with unexpected angles.

'I hope quittin's a choice after today, Marshal. I shorely do.'

The marshal let out an uneasy laugh. 'You an' me both. I gotta be a damn fool gettin' involved in this over nothin'.'

Banner felt his belly tighten. 'What do you mean "nothin"?'

The marshal looked at his saddle and Banner's face grew dark. 'Ain't no gold in this shipment, Banner.'

'What the hell you mean, no gold?'

'Nephew pulled the shipment and sent it on another stage. Swapped it with a supply shipment that was s'posed to travel two days from now.'

'Got a hell of a lot of faith in us, don't he?' The announcement didn't surprise Banner in the least, except for the fact that the nephew had had the brains to think of it in the first place.

'You blame 'im? Red Widow Gang ain't 'xactly got a reputation for missin' what they aim for.'

'Reckon they don't. Just means we best put an end to it today so it won't be for nothin', then. Can't say I'm happy about it, but it don't make a lick of difference. Gang still needs to be taken care of and that's what we're here for.'

The marshal nodded. 'Knew you'd see it that way so I didn't bother to tell you.'

'Wouldn't have changed things any . . .' Banner muttered, wondering if maybe it might have, if maybe he would have decided it was foolish to risk his life for an empty stage and gone back to the hotel and taken Cynthia up on her offer.

No, he still saw no choice. The gang would still be after him for some reason known only to themselves and he still had to put a stop to them before they did to him.

The marshal let out a grunt. 'Hell, what made Zellers so sure they'd find out about the shipment and hit this stage anyhow?'

Banner sighed. 'Man like Zellers didn't get where he got by being anyone's patsy. He musta had a strong notion they'd discover that shipment was coming in. Gang has a way of finding out things about his stages; they been hittin' them regular-like.'

'What if they find out there ain't no gold on this stage?'

'Last minute switch. . . .' Banner shook his head. 'Ain't likely. They might suspect the move, but wouldn't risk passing it up in case they were wrong. And they got no qualms 'bout killin' so it don't make no never-mind to them.'

The sound of hoofbeats suddenly took their attention and their gazes turned towards the trail ahead. A rider galloped along, dust billowing around his bay's beating hooves, dirt spewing backwards. The deputy reined to a halt in front of Banner and the marshal.

Catching his breath, the deputy said, 'They're comin', 'bout a mile back. Takin' their time 'bout it, too.'

Banner nodded and they guided their horses down the slope onto the trail. Within minutes the sound of clattering iron tyres rattled from the distance, and to Banner it sounded like a dirge. Maybe it was. A death song for a man who had lived with too many demons for too many years. His thoughts again went to Cynthia in the hotel room. He pushed them away, knowing it would do no good to dwell on it at this point and would only distract him from the job at hand. He couldn't afford that, not if he intended to return to her without looking like a sluice box.

The stage rounded the bend and he watched one of the drivers urge the horses to a halt. The man nodded at the marshal and Banner, face grim and sweat streaming from his forehead. The stage door popped open and one of the men jumped out, looking a whole lot more relieved than the one who was staying, Banner reckoned.

'You Hart and Banner?' the man asked.

The marshal's brow scrunched. 'Hell of a question. If we weren't, you'd be spoutin' your innards.'

The man nodded, mild annoyance dancing in his dusty eyes. 'You got a point.' He tipped his hat at Banner. 'Heard a lot about you, fella. Anyone can put an end to these scalawags you can.'

Banner grimaced, a bit embarrassed by the man's assessment. He climbed from his sorrel and handed the reins to the guard. Drawing his Peacemaker, he double-checked its readiness then reholstered it. He knew the pistol had a full belly, but he needed the ritual of the thing, though it provided damn little comfort. He glanced at the stage, wondering if he weren't taking a ride into certain death. Cynthia's face rose in his mind and he felt a twinge of dread, but walked towards the stage, face grim and soul heavy.

'Banner, you take care, now,' he heard Marshal Hart say behind him, but didn't respond. Words were useless and he needed to summon every ounce of focus he had if he were going to keep his promise to Cynthia Addleson.

He climbed inside and tugged the door closed. The guard sitting across from him nodded. 'Most likely spot for 'em to hit us is about a mile outside town. There's a congested area around the trail with lots of brush and trees. Plenty of hiding space for 'em. If it's gonna happen it'll happen then.'

The manhunter nodded, mouth drawing into a tight line. He agreed. He knew the place and it was perfect for an ambush. Besides brush and trees, strewn boulders and deadfall littered the low hills. He glanced at the Winchester propped against the seat and took it in his hands; it scarcely felt comforting. More out of needing something to do than uncertainty, he checked its load and prayed he'd get the chance to use it.

One of the drivers shouted 'Yah!' and the stage started forward. He glanced outside, watching the marshal, guard and deputy fall back.

You're riding into Hell, Banner and you know it. And goddamn if the Devil ain't gonna be there to welcome you. . . .

He took a deep breath, feeling every bone shudder with each bump the iron tyres didn't miss. The rutted trail provided plenty of opportunity for bumps and the inexperienced drivers seemed intent on hitting every damn one of them. They were merely guards and he wondered if the advantage wasn't lost by having two of them. An experienced driver would know better how to maneuver the contraption and work the horses, perhaps avoid something the man driving now wouldn't. He let out a low grunt. Hell, maybe it didn't matter, because that would only put an innocent man at risk and the Red Widow Gang didn't exactly have a record of failure.

Their speed picked up and Banner felt his nerves cinch all the more. He scanned the terrain outside, picking out every possible hiding place, searching for any hint of sunlight glinting from a gun barrel or movement of black and red. He saw nothing, but that was to be expected.

He shot a glance at the man sitting across from him and noticed the fellow's face had pinched tight as a whore's corset. The guard looked young, hardly more than a boy and Banner had heard a nervous hitch in the man's voice that didn't please him in the least.

The man made movements with his mouth then said, 'Got me a new wife at home, mister.' The hitch in his voice had turned into a tremor. Banner felt something in his belly sink and cursed men like the dead stage owner for being so generous with other folks' lives.

'What the goddamn hell you doin' on this stage, then, son?' His voice carried no condemnation, but maybe something as close to concern as he ever expressed. For a moment he thought of Jamie, then Cynthia, and cursed his own choices.

'Reckon I had me no choice. Was the only job I could git and I got her in a family way, sir.'

Banner sighed and shook his head, wondering if things could get any worse, knowing damn well they could. Besides the obvious fool-heartery of leaving a new wife and unborn child behind, this man might hesitate out of fear for his own life, unlike a more seasoned guard or manhunter. That might assure the fellow's death, and perhaps the demise of the rest, too. Banner would keep a careful eye on the fella and hoped it wouldn't throw off his focus.

The stage suddenly shuddered and a deafening boom stopped all other sound.

The concussion clouted the stage and Banner was hurled from his seat, barely able to keep himself from colliding with the fellow in the opposite seat by thrusting out his arms and slamming his hands against the stage wall. He lost the Winchester; it clattered on the floor without discharging.

The guard slammed backward against the stage wall and lost his own rifle. His eyes tumbled up into his head then dropped down again.

Outside, frantic neighing filled the air and Banner distantly heard it, the noise of the explosion still ringing in his ears. The stage bounced and careened suddenly forward as the frightened team bolted.

Banner pushed himself backward and landed in his seat. He realized instantly what had happened and cursed himself. While focusing on the other man, he had not been looking outside and at that moment, by luck or providence, the Red Widow Gang had struck. He reckoned one of them had hurled a stick of dynamite, but had misjudged the timing slightly and the explosion had come from behind. That stuck him as downright strange and wholly inefficient for a gang who had terrorized the area and never come up short in a robbery.

The stage careened forward, hitting each dip and rise, rattling, jouncing, crashing down dangerously. He wondered how much the thing would take before it shook itself to pieces. He heard the horses' thundering hooves and frightened bleats, the driver's frantic yells and curses, as they struggled to control the terrified animals.

The young guard was rubbing the back of his head, conscious but looking stunned. Banner fished on the floor for both rifles, shoving one at the guard. His gaze snapped to the outside; scenery streamed by, but he saw nothing and reckoned the gang must be behind them.

A bullet struck the side of the stage, confirming his notion. Splinters spiraled away from the door. Banner jumped from his seat, crouching, urging the guard to do the same. The man seemed too dazed to comprehend and didn't move.

'Get down 'fore they blow your damn fool head off, goddammit!' Banner shouted, grabbing the man's arm and yanking him to the floor. The fellow's face suddenly twisted with terror and he clutched to his rifle for dear life.

Banner could do nothing now except ride it out and that gave him a damn uneasy feeling. He was used to more control on cases. This was new to him and only his years' worth of manhunting experience kept him from panicking like the young guard.

Three more bullets spanged into the side of the stage and he felt damn lucky none had punched through and hit them. It was almost as if the bandits, however many there were, were missing on purpose, simply trying to stop the stage. But that was impossible and useless. They would not care what condition it was in as long as it was halted, period. They wanted the gold, nothing else, except maybe the death of all aboard and a well-aimed piece of dynamite would serve that end all the better.

As if in taunt, another explosion boomed. The stage jerked. This blast came from further back, but the concussion still rattled the buggy. A volley of shots followed, most missing, a few thunking into the stage.

A heart beat. Two. He heard a sudden *crack!* and his belly dropped.

'Judas Priest . . .' Banner mumbled. The stage jerked, canted left and dipped. Banner knew with grim certainty the crack had been the sound of the iron tyre snapping off. Metal and wood skidding over hard-packed ground made a horrendous shrieking as the frightened horses dragged the stage forward despite the missing wheel. Sparks fanned up in a shower of yellow and gold.

Banner heard the drivers' curses grow louder and more vulgar as they desperately fought for control of the team.

The contraption slowed but was tilting more and more left. A vague panic hit him as he realized something would have to give – the stage or the horses; neither prospect was particularly appealing.

Suddenly the stage bucked and sent him sprawling to the floor. A beat later another loud crack came and the back end dropped and slammed into the ground.

The man with him now looked more petrified than most conscious men could be, and that worried him damn near as much as the fact that he knew both wheels had come off the stage.

He grabbed the guard's arms, shaking him. 'Listen to me! Any second this stage is going to come apart, you understand? The horses will keep pullin' it and the front wheels are going to give. If we're in it. . . .'

The man, though terrified, jerkily nodded his understanding. The stage slowed as the horses strained to drag its weight. It wasn't enough, but Banner knew they had no choice. They had only fractions of seconds left.

He forced himself to his feet and kicked open the door. Immediately lead punched holes in it. Banner felt his belly sink.

'Jump!' he shouted at the guard but the man froze, too panicked to move. Banner backhanded him and the fellow got a measure of his gumption back. 'Goddammit, jump or you'll never see that baby born!'

He grabbed the man and hurled him forward and out, praying the fellow would land with his senses enough intact not to break every bone in his body nor get struck by a well-aimed bullet. It was a risk Banner had to take; remaining in the stage meant certain death.

Banner flung himself out into space a beat later.

He felt suspended in the air, floating, and the thought flashed through his mind he presented a perfect target for the gang. He expected lead to drill into his body at any instant, but none came. He hit the ground hard, air exploding from his lungs, and rolled with the impact. He lost his grip on the Winchester, which went flying to his left.

He kept rolling, not wanting to present any target worth taking a bead on. The woodland whirled past his vision. Dirt clogged his mouth, and he tasted blood as his teeth clacked together, puncturing his lip in the process.

Slowing, he came up on hands and knees. He immediately scuttled forward, towards a sheltering boulder.

A shriek snapped his attention left and he saw the guard he had shoved out first rising and staring straight ahead. The man had lost his rifle as well and was struggling to pull his Colt out of its holster.

Banner spotted the reason for his fright. A rider bore down on him from the side, a rider garbed in black, a red poncho draped over his shoulders. A black mask covered the fellow's face. The bandit was levering a Smith & Wesson on the guard, who appeared suddenly frozen in mid-draw.

Banner saw death flash in the young guard's eyes. The fellow could do nothing in time to prevent the bandit from sending him to Boot Hill and leaving a woman a widow with a child to rear on her own.

But while the guard could do nothing to prevent his fate, Luke Banner could.

The speed and reflexes had slipped a notch, but what remained was enough to serve his end.

His hand swept for his Peacemaker, grasping the butt and drawing it in one fluid motion. Levelling. Feathering the trigger.

A shot blasted and the bandit jolted, kicked backward off his horse. The bay kept going and the hardcase slammed into the ground on his back, unmoving, chest gouting blood. For once Banner reckoned he had no regrets about killing a man. At least he wouldn't if the guard recovered from his shock and got himself clear of trouble.

'Get down, you damn fool!' Banner shouted, motioning towards the fellow. The guard came unfrozen and bolted for the cover of a tree. Banner had saved him momentarily but God knew if it would be enough.

A number of things seemed to happen at once. Ahead the stage parted from its wheels and crashed into the ground with a horrendous clatter and shrieking.

The guards leaped from the drivers' box an instant before and flew in opposite directions. They hit the ground rolling, then sprang to their feet and scrambled for cover.

The stage broke apart, boards flying like wooden rain. Trunks of supposed gold exploded open as they hit the hard-pack, spewing clothes and pulp novels and blankets. The horses bleated and kept hurtling forward, towing their traces, vanishing down the trail in a cloud of dust and whinnies and frantic hoofbeats.

Banner's gaze jumped towards the bandits, eight of them he counted at a glance, all galloping in from behind and to the left. Holding the advantage, they were swarming in for the kill.

The young guard, ensconced behind a tree, seemed to have no desire to fire back as the bandits triggered shots and riddled the area with bullets. Clomps of dirt flew up and bark splintered from trees. The air turned acrid with blue smoke.

A guard tried to fire at one of the bandits and got a bullet between his eyes for his trouble. The man fell backwards like a tree going down and Banner felt suddenly sickened.

He raised his Colt and plucked the bandit from his saddle. He wasn't sure where he had hit him but the man landed hard enough head first to crack his skull and no longer pose a problem.

Two down, six to go and Banner had one guard terrified and not firing, and only one other man and himself until the marshal, deputy and remaining guard arrived.

A bullet spanged from the boulder, chipping stone, and Banner ducked back. He swung his Peacemaker, firing two more times and nailing another bandit, but not enough to stop him.

The other driver popped up and squeezed off two shots, finishing the job and the bandit hit the ground, unmoving.

The driver kept firing, emptying his gun then reloading and firing some more. Banner didn't think he was even aiming, just frightened and pulling the trigger hoping to hit something, anything.

The bandits swerved around, angling left and right and Banner knew they were trying to surround them. The Red Widows hunched low, no longer presenting easy targets now that they knew Banner and the guard still had firepower left.

A thought invaded Banner's mind: The gang might not have expected the return fire but they suddenly seemed to have become damned inefficient. Whatever the reason, Banner had no time to dwell on it and pumped more shots.

Bullets came with increasing fury and a sudden shriek tore from the driver's lips. The man stumbled from behind cover, a spot just over his heart spurting blood. That was the last of him. A volley of bullets jerked his body right then left like a ragdoll and finally kicked him backward. He lay on the ground, riddled, blood soaking into the soil.

For all intents and purposes Banner was alone, the remaining guard useless in the fight. He saw no way to fight off five bandits though one marauder was open and if he were going to go down he was going to take another of the bastards with him.

He stepped around the boulder, drawing a bead on the one who had just riddled the guard with lead. The bandit was only partly open, leaning half over his horse, fully confident his fellow robbers were covering him and he was likely right. Banner was risking everything, now, but he had no choice. He would be gunned down anyway.

A sudden pounding of hooves came from the trail and Banner's head twisted. He spotted the deputy, marshal and the other guard careening around the bend. The exposed bandit saw them, too. He hesitated a fraction and Banner fired. The man grasped his shoulder and bellowed a curse. Banner squeezed off another shot, sending the man hurtling backward off his horse.

There was a moment of suspended fire then bullets flew in earnest, volley after volley coming from bandits and lawmen alike. Clouds of blue smoke drifted across the trail and the thunder of gunfire grew deafening.

Something's wrong. . . .

The firing ceased. Banner started to turn, an icy sensation washing through his body. Now he knew why the other bandit hadn't been afraid of partially exposing himself – another gang member had maneuvered directly behind Banner. Gunshots had covered the sound of the horse edging up.

The black and red figure, like some nightmarish representation of Death, levered a Smith & Wesson at Banner's chest. He could not get his gun around in time. He would die and the only things that flashed through his mind then was Cynthia Addleson's face and a broken promise.

The figure did an odd thing. It hesitated. Banner kept turning. The gun was directly on him and a simple squeeze would end his life.

But the bandit didn't fire.

A blast sounded from nearby. The Red Widow member tried to spin, half-way made it before a bullet punched into its shoulder. The figure jolted, arching straight up in the saddle.

Banner glanced right and saw the marshal levering his Colt for the finishing shot.

The bandit managed to keep a grip on the pommel and twist, sending the bullet meant for Banner in Hart's direction. The lawman jerked, then doubled, a slug ploughing into his side.

The lawdog squeezed off another shot as he buckled and a second bullet slammed into the Red Widow Gang member. This time it took the figure in the upper thigh and the horse jolted and reared. The figure barely managed to hold on, slipping to the side, leg caught in a stirrup, which prevented the robber from falling to the ground, as the horse slammed down and bolted.

As the horse galloped away, Banner tried to get his gun around in time to finish off the killer. He fired but a dull clack sounded. His gun was empty and even if he had been able to fire on the bandit in the first place he would have been caught dead.

You've gone over the hill. That one was enough to finish you. . . .

The horse picked up speed and angled onto the hard-packed trail, disappearing in a cloud of dust and receding hoofbeats.

Banner stepped back behind the boulder, whirling, no time to worry about one escaped bandit. He quickly reloaded, but it was too late.

Heavy silence had fallen and he saw bodies lying everywhere. The marshal was doubled over in his saddle and the bandits were all sprawled along the ground, except for the one who had gotten away. The deputy appeared unscathed, but the guard was dead and Banner didn't care much for the morbid irony of that. The man had been relieved not to be riding on the stage, yet he was dead and Banner was alive. Hell of a note.

Banner reckoned he'd now have one more ghost haunting him.

It was over. The Red Widow gang was vanquished and likely one escaped member, wounded, perhaps mortally, wouldn't cause a problem. He went to the marshal, who was straightening in his saddle, a pained look twisting his face.

Banner gazed up at him, grimness turning his own features. 'You hit bad?'

The marshal shook his head. 'Didn't hit no vitals, but sure took a bit of tallow.' He tried a smile and climbed from his horse, shaky at first, but steadying after a moment, gripping his side.

Banner holstered his gun. The surroundings suddenly seemed deathly silent, somber, as they always did after death visited. The Red Widow gang was no more and Banner would join them at least to all concerned. He would have the marshal and deputy tell the papers and any who asked that he had perished in the gunfight. His name would become the stuff of legends, heralded in death as a hero for bringing down a notorious gang and dying for the cause of justice.

The last draw for a manhunter who had likely always been looking to die. Now he would.

Banner turned, the somberness sinking deep into him, and he went towards the young guard, who had finally come from his hiding place. He saw tears on the man's face and if there were anything Banner felt thankful for it was the fact this man would be going back to his family.

'You go home, son.' Banner's gaze drilled the man. 'Ride out and never look back and find yourself another line of work. You won't live long you keep ridin' this trail.'

The man nodded and walked past Banner, looking embarrassed and relieved at the same time. Banner stared off in the direction the wounded bandit had taken, wondering if the fellow would make it very far before he lost too much blood.

He turned, starting back to his horse. There was nothing else to do. He would go back to Cynthia, now, keep his promise and pray she would still have a man who had risked everything to put a demon to rest.

You still don't know why they wanted you dead. . . .

No, he did not, and none of them here was left alive to tell. He doubted the escaped one would be found alive. The reason he had been lured to Bellstar would have to remain a mystery. It didn't please him but there was damn little he could do about it.

He stopped and a chill washed through him. A glint of something had caught his eye and he knelt, plucking at a metal object embedded into a hoofprint in the ground, thinking the marshal or deputy had lost his badge. He pulled it free, turning it over in his hand and suddenly curling his fingers tightly over it. His hand bleached, tendons standing out as he squeezed, and he didn't move. His head dropped and something inside him seemed to wither.

'Banner?' he heard the marshal say, as the lawman came up to him.

Luke Banner didn't answer. A tear slid down his face and somewhere from his past a ghost laughed.

TEN

The doorknob turned and Luke Banner looked up from where he was sitting on the edge of the bed in Cynthia Addleson's hotel room. His heart pounded in his throat and he swallowed, waiting for the door to open. It had come down to this, a turn he never expected and desperately didn't want. The end. Of everything. Not just of Luke Banner, but of some distant dream he hadn't known existed in the first place and by God he reckoned that was harder to lose.

The door clicked and Banner's teeth clenched, balls of muscle standing out on either side of his jaw. He tightly clutched the object he had discovered at the site of the ambush, afraid somehow to open his hand and prove this wasn't just some horrible nightmare.

But it was no dream, though certainly a nightmare. A waking nightmare. It was fact. And now it needed to be dealt with in a final tally, one where no mistakes could be allowed; he had made too goddamn many over the last few days. The reason he'd been lured here was all too clear to him now: a loose end, what he had always feared, had caught up with him.

You were a fool, Banner. You were deceived by the oldest of games. . . .

The door swung inward and a figure dressed in

148

black and red stepped inside, halting instantly as it saw him. Banner didn't stir, simply waited. A gunbelt encircled the bandit's hips.

The figure eased the door shut then didn't move.

Banner's lips turned with a grim expression. He lifted his closed hand and slowly opened his fingers, letting the silver locket in his palm fall onto the bed beside him, where there as also a small pile of business cards, a square of sealing wax and stamp.

'I opened the locket. . . .' His words came low and heavy with regret, pain. 'The man inside . . . he was one of the men who killed Jamie. . . .'

The figure remained still for a moment, then its hand went to the mask covering its face and pulled it free. Blonde hair tumbled out across the red poncho draped over Cynthia Addleson's shoulders.

Removing her gloves and letting them drop to the floor she gave a grim smile and Banner saw something different about her immediately, something cold and vacant. 'I knew when I discovered I lost it you would find it and be waiting.' Her words came strained and suddenly her hand went to her thigh. Banner saw blood run between her fingers and drip onto the floor from the wound delivered by the marshal. It didn't look serious, but she was losing blood and if it weren't treated infection would set in. She had also been hit in the shoulder, but that one appeared not to be bleeding.

'Who was he?' Banner stood, but did not come forward.

Cynthia gave a humorless laugh. 'He was my brother. I told you he died at a creek. You killed him, Luke. He was all I had and you killed him. I was so young.'

'He was a killer.' Banner took a step forward, drawing a deep breath. 'He murdered Jamie and tried to kill me. I had no choice.'

'I know. . . .' Her voice lowered and deep pain drifted across her eyes. 'He raised me to be the same way, taught me how to shoot and take what I wanted, needed – taught me how to kill. I spent all my time alone after he died, perfecting my skills until they were as good as I knew yours would be.'

'Your sister?'

She laughed. 'I never had one. Never had me a goddamn dress shop neither, though I did spend plenty of time back East learnin' how to talk right, though hell if I could keep it up.'

Banner felt his insides twisting as he stared into the face of the woman he had fallen in love with, the woman he now knew to be the leader of the Red Widow Gang.

'You sent the money, called me here?'

She nodded, a wince taking her face and she gripped her thigh tighter. 'Yes, I did. You see I waited, Luke, waited all that time just for the moment I would have you. Then I tested you, hired Trombley to kill you. I knew he would never beat you. Even drunk you would be too much for him, but I have to admit I was surprised how close he came. That would have ruined everything, though.'

'Test me?'

'You see I needed to know just what I was up against, how fast you really were, if you had slipped at all. I've followed your career from the day you killed my brother, Luke. I read everything in pulp novels and newspapers, and even followed you a few times. I was in October Creek and watched you for a day or two, then sent the message to your agency and transferred the retainer.'

'Why didn't you just kill me when I came here, or even back then?'

She laughed. 'You ain't an easy man to kill, Luke. You got a knack for survivin'. And I wanted to kill you myself, make you pay for killing my brother. I decided to get close to you, close enough to make you let your guard down and make it easy for me.'

Banner's gaze dropped and came back up, sorrow coming in waves as what was left of his world collapsed. He saw the woman before him now in clear light, a conniving manipulating hardcase bent on revenge, in some ways so much like himself, yet in others so very different. They were both creatures driven by a dark demon, but now his was gone, some-how. It had died and he reckoned it would take years to figure out just how. She had a lot to do with it, despite his discovery, and that couldn't be changed.

'Your man tried to kill me in the alley. . . .'

'Another test, one I knew you'd easily pass. You were better that time, I must admit. I knew then it would take more work than I thought to soften you up. . . .'

'Lead me into your web . . .' Banner whispered.

'Yes, lead you into my web. You know what a widow spider does after she mates, Luke?'

He nodded, understanding the grim way she had been thinking and cursing himself for being so easy to fool. He had spent so many years alone and Cynthia Addleson had taken full advantage of that fact, told him everything he'd needed to hear, *wanted* to hear. 'They kill their mates. . . .'

She nodded. 'That's right, Luke. And that's what I planned to do with you, kill you after you fell asleep after we made love.'

'Your man at Zellers' nephew's place almost got me, so did the one in the doc's. More tests?'

She gave a laugh that had a measure of insanity to it. 'No, no . . . I didn't expect you to be there. Didn't reckon you'd take Zellers' job so fast.'

'But you knew I would take it?'

'Yes, I knew. I could see everything in your eyes, Luke. There was nothing you could hide from me the way you did others. You weren't s'posed to be there and by the time I got near the place the marshal had already killed Henkins. I would have killed him myself if he hadn't.'

'And at the doc's?'

'He was acting on his own. I never would have sent him to kill you dressed as a Red Widow. It linked us to the reason you were here. You did me a favor by killin' him.'

Banner hesitated, swallowing at the emotion jammed in his throat. He had been taken in by this woman, by some need he had not known existed any more and he couldn't allow that to happen again.

'You missed me on purpose at the marshal's yesterday – it was you on that rooftop, wasn't it?'

She nodded. 'Yes, it was me. I could have easily hit you if I wanted to. I don't miss when I aim.'

'And today, when you had me dead in your sights you didn't fire. You could have ended it right there, taken your revenge and that would have been that.'

She laughed, the sound rising in pitch. 'Don't you understand, Luke? I could have killed you any time I wanted to. I could have killed you last night after you fell asleep, way I planned. I never did fall asleep, Luke. I pretended to, but I was awake, waiting. It would have been so easy a number of times.'

He shook his head, thoughts jumbled. 'Why didn't you kill me? That's what you brought me here to do.'

She peered at him and for a moment a trace of the

old Cynthia came back, the warmth in her sapphire eyes. 'Because I fell in love with you, Luke. I knew it from the moment I saw the darkness in your eyes; you were just like me and I had been lonely for so long. You were a kindred spirit and after you told me about her death I knew things weren't so clear, so cut and dried. I set out to trap you in a mistake, the mistake of falling in love with a deadly creature, and fell into it myself. That's why I didn't kill you last night. I shot at you to scare you off the case, stop you from going after the Red Widows as I knew you would.'

'Surely you knew that wouldn't scare me off?'

'I knew, but I had to try. I was going to come to you later, convince you to make love to me and go away together. That's why when you showed up here yesterday I knew I had you completely, or thought I did until you told me you were going after them anyway.'

'You could have stopped the robbery today. . . .'

'Could I? I had a man inside Zellers' company. We planned that stage hit from the moment he found out it was comin'. Everything was set; it would be hit on time in that precise spot. My men would be in position and had orders to strike if something went wrong and I didn't show up. I was fully convinced I could make you come with me and let the Red Widow Gang perish in that robbery. It would be over then and I knew without my direction they would make foolish mistakes. If any survived they would scatter.'

'But you went with them?'

'Yes. Because I knew you would be killed in the attempt and I couldn't have that. You see, though I loved you and wanted you to come with me, if you were to die it had to be by my hand. There was no other way. You'd come with me somehow, or die – we both would.'

He saw it coming then, caught a certain tenseness to her words that translated to her muscles. Every gunfighter had it and he reckoned he probably did too, but most couldn't read it. He could. The intent of the draw. The beginning. The end.

Her hand was suddenly sweeping towards the Smith & Wesson at her hip.

He could not get his Peacemaker out before she drew and fired, though his hand was already whisking towards it to try. Cynthia Addleson would get what she had wanted for years – Luke Banner's death.

Then something happened. Her eyes flashed to his and her hand hesitated the merest fraction of time, allowing him to reach his Peacemaker at the same moment she clutched her gun. He knew right then she had fallen insanely in love with him, snared in her own trap, a woman driven by darkness and desperation and loneliness, vulnerable in a way she could never have known. The same way as he. And what had prevented her from killing him today nearly stopped her now. But not quite.

Her gun came up.

So did his.

Both weapons seemed linked, rising together, shots thundering at the same instant, reports blending as though only one had been fired.

A burning jolt kicked Banner backwards and he went down. He hit the floor hard, flat on his back. He stared up at the ceiling, which began to shimmer and blur. Warm liquid trickled down his side and he knew it was blood.

It all came together in a flash, his life, the darkness inside him, the hope and falling apart of his dreams and future. He had slipped too much, gone on just a fraction too long, as all his kind did. He had been a fool again, for not the first time in his life, but he reckoned the last.

Then darkness invaded from the corner of his mind, sweeping in in soft shadowed waves, and before it enveloped him completely he whispered Jamie's name.

'Ashes to ashes. . . .' The preacher's voice droned low and somber and Marshal Hart looked down at the small stone bearing the name Luke Banner. He and the deputy, along with the preacher, were gathered in the wooded cemetery at the edge of town. A gaggle of local newspapermen and a number of scribes from surrounding towns who had come as soon as the news of Banner's death spread, peered anxiously at the grave, scribbling on their pads with expressions that said more about the stories they were envisioning than the death of a fellow human being. They wanted to make a spectacle of it but Hart had thwarted most of that. Still he could not prevent what would be written in accounts and pulp novels, but he reckoned that was not his job. He had done the best he could.

The day had turned to grey, slate clouds scribbled with charcoal sliding in from the west, auguring storms. Splotches of rain splashed occasionally on the headstone.

The preacher babbled on, most of the words lost on Marshal Hart, then closed the book, glancing at the lawdog, who nodded. The marshal shifted, still aching in his side, though the new doctor had removed the bullet days ago.

'I didn't know Luke Banner long,' said the marshal, voice somber. 'Reckon I knew him well enough, though, at least to count him as a friend and a hell of a man. Weren't for him the Red Widow Gang would still be killin' and if he had to die he died a hero's death.

Reckon the West won't be quite as safe without him.'

'Amen,' muttered the preacher, nodding and looking thankful it was over. Hart set his hat back on his head and glanced at the reporters, who were still scribbling furiously with stubs of pencil on their note-pads.

'Reckon you fellas got what you came for. Appreciate it if you'd let the man rest in peace now and take your circus out of town.'

The scribes glanced at each other and nodded, but Hart saw it in their eyes: this was big news and would be splashed all over the headlines in the biggest letters possible. Hell, what did it matter, though? Luke Banner was dead, though his legend would live on and Hart prayed that would be the end of it. God knew, however, some fools didn't have the courtesy to stay dead. . . .

'Right nice words you said 'bout me, Marshal,' said Luke Banner as Hart stepped around a huge cottonwood. Banner was leaning back-to against the tree, his thoughts laced with sadness and a burning pain in his side where the new doc had patched up the hole left by Cynthia Addleson's bullet. An expert shot, the lead had punched clean through and hit nothing vital, though he had lost a goodly amount of blood before the marshal found him lying on the floor in the hotel room. Many times since that day he wished the marshal had just left him there to die with her.

His bullet had landed a bit more true, drilling deep into her heart. She had died instantly and for that he should have been glad. But he wasn't. All he had was a profound sense of sadness and grief and promises unfulfilled.

And more ghosts.

'Glad you liked 'em,' said Hart, removing his hat.

'Just see to it you got the goddamn sense to stay in your grave.' He grinned but there was no humor in it.

Banner nodded, staring up at the distant grey sky. 'You buried her proper?'

The marshal nodded. 'Yeah, I did, despite my better judgement. Don't see why you want someone like that treated so respectfully.'

Banner uttered a sharp grunt. 'Death changes us sometimes, Marshal, makes us something we're not. Whatever Cynthia Addleson was, she carried a speck of light inside her. I saw it and I believe she missed killing me on purpose at the very last.'

The marshal shook his head and gave a disgusted *pfft*. 'How can you say that, Banner? She led a gang of bandits and was a vicious killer. And she tried to kill you more than once.'

Banner nodded, knowing the man was right, but something inside him couldn't let her go without at least a proper burial. 'Sometimes I ain't so sure she was any worse than me, Marshal.'

'Oh, pshaw! It's a matter of sides, Banner. You on the right and her on the wrong. We're all touched by death, especially out here, but we all don't become killers or innocent folk. You might have seen some light in her and you might damn well go to your real grave thinkin' she intended to not kill you at the last, but I don't believe it for a minute. She was wounded and that's all it was that made her miss.'

Banner nodded. Maybe Hart was right, but he couldn't help wondering, though he reckoned it didn't matter. For she had reaped what she sowed and that was that. Except for a place deep inside hlm where the small hope she had turned loose still lived.

The marshal fished in a pocket and brought out a shiny object, peering at it a moment then handing it to

Banner. 'Didn't bury it with her. Figured you might want it.'

The manhunter took it, the locket that had belonged to Cynthia. Curling his fingers over it, he swallowed hard at the emotion choking his throat.

'Obliged, Marshal.' It was all he could say, maybe all that needed saying.

'You won't change your mind, will you, Banner?' the marshal asked, concern on his face.

Banner shook his head. 'No, the world needs to know Luke Banner is dead. It's the only way. I've lost the edge, Marshal. Cynthia Addleson proved that. I could always tell when men were deceiving me, when something wasn't right. It's the vital skill a manhunter has, least a good one who stays alive. I missed it with her, let my feelings and restlessness get in the way. I went over the hill all at once and I somehow got lucky enough to escape the fate most gunfighters meet. Next time . . . well, it would be the last time because it would kill me.'

'You sure that ain't what you still want?' The marshal eyed him suspiciously.

Banner grinned half-heartedly. 'Maybe, but it will come at a time of my choosing.'

'You can't control death like you did hardcases, Banner. Just recollect that.'

'Can't I? I have so far.'

'That's just the kinda talk that'll get you planted for real.'

'Reckon you're right.' He laughed, little emotion in it.

'You loved her, didn't you?' The marshal's face turned softer, a sadness in his eyes.

'Reckon. As much as a man like me can love.' He wasn't being quite honest, but what the hell. 'Maybe it was just the years alone, having no place to call my own, no ties. All men deserve that, Marshal.'

'Even you, Banner.'

He nodded. 'Even me.'

The marshal sighed and set his hat back on his head. 'Stay alive, Banner. Stay true to your word and start that ranch and if you can love again, do it.'

Banner smiled a grim smile. 'But Luke Banner's already dead, Marshal.'

The marshal shook his head and clasped Banner's hand then walked away. Banner stared back at his headstone a hundred feet distant then went to his horse and mounted. He tucked the locket into the pocket above his heart and a single tear strolled down his face.

Rain began to fall, dribbling over the rim of his hat and soaking his clothes but he paid it no mind. He rode at an easy trot into the grey day, never once looking back to see if any of the ghosts had followed. . . .